G000230600

The Caterpillar Club

The Caterpillar Club

Mark Rae

MARK'S MUSIC

First published in Great Britain 2021
by Mark's Music
49 Errington Road, Ponteland,
Newcastle Upon Tyne, NE20 9LB.

This novel has an accompanying soundtrack, it is available
on vinyl and CD. The double pack CD contains an ambient
readers' version which is intended to be played while the book is read.
This version may also be listened to on streaming services such as
Spotify, Apple Music and Amazon Music.

https://markrae.bandcamp.com/

A CIP catalogue record for this book is available from the
British Library.

ISBN (Hardback) 978-1-8384128-0-7
ISBN (Export Trade Paperback) 978-1-8384128-1-4
ISBN (eBook) 978-1-8384128-2-1

Printed in Great Britain by Clays Ltd, Elcograf S.p.A

FSC
www.fsc.org
MIX
Paper from
responsible sources
FSC® C018072

For Angie, Henry, Christine & Jack

1

The End of The Night

It's 9:45 on Saturday night. Simon lifts his record boxes from the boot of the taxi onto the cold oily tarmac of Portobello Road. The brake lights of the Prius cast a glow over the stickers covering the record boxes. Simon thanks the driver as a baby cries for a parent through an open window up high on the other side of the road. He slips his hands into the worn leather handles of the record boxes and lifts them with an exhale, his body swaying up to the green entrance door of the Ilithios Members Club.

"Yes, DJ," the six-foot-four Ghanaian doorman in a long grey Crombie greets him, his deep voice rattling the cold winter air.

Simon nods his respect in return, his slim unshaven face lit up blue in the neon sign. The doorman presses a buzzer, the lock clicks and Simon steps on the bottom of the door.

Inside the cramped entrance of the club the smell of cologne hangs like liquid money in the warm air. Up the narrow stairs he lugs the ancient cargo, the muscles in his thighs burning with each step. Thin corridors greet each new floor, spilling a splatter of piercing sound into his ringing ears. The chink of glass on glass, the false guffaws of high society conversation and the hurried orders of the staff firing fast in Romanian, Polish and Italian. He stops to catch his breath in an empty alcove and texts his wife, Sonia, to let her know he's arrived at the venue.

Simon has to climb three flights of stairs to get to the library room at the top of the building. A teak bar finished with polished brass has a DJ booth fashioned from an oak table with ornately carved legs. The library room is lit low and fitted with old leather furniture refurbished at great expense, polished up and positioned in its dark recesses. Shapely lights finished with bronze and golden tassels are attached to the walls at head height. The library bookcase is filled with a dead DJ's record collection; no one remembers his name. Any personal information has been lost with the turnover of staff. "The brother of someone who put cash into The Ministry of Sound," was as far as Simon got after asking one of the staff.

Simon situates himself behind the decks and readies to settle into his rhythm. He starts by fixing the mess left by the DJ who played last night. The EQs are boosted to the limit and the master volume twisted round as far as it will go. A member's birthday party was held in the library room earlier in the evening and a live lobster is sitting on ice in a bucket next to the bookcase, with its mandibles foaming. Behind the creature the JB's album "Food for Thought" is hanging out of the vinyl collection.

"What's going on over here then?" Simon asks his favourite member of staff, Patryk, who is dressed in suit pants and a waistcoat.

"I don't know. They didn't want the lobster," Patryk answers in his heavy Polish accent.

"What a waste," Simon tuts before peeling off a faded burgundy jumper to reveal his black short-sleeved work shirt, still damp from the climb up the stairs. "She's still alive and she's berried."

"Berried?" The barman raises his brow.

"Eggs, Patryk. She's curling her tail like that to protect her eggs." Simon shapes his fingers into a curl.

"Don't worry. They'll move it before they let the customers up." Patryk continues to shine the glassware piled up next to the DJ equipment.

"I don't care about the customers, Patryk. If we were closer to the sea, I'd run and let her go," Simon says, pointing to where he imagines the Thames meets the North Sea.

The members are slowly arriving, dressed at great expense. The first three hours of the job are easy. Everyone talks in the downstairs bar out of sight. Simon plays his own demos mixed with songs he wants to hear until around 1 a.m. when the manager comes thundering out of the darkness in his black work shirt, like a clockwork Mussolini.

"They want a party downstairs," he shouts with his arms flailing.

"If you give me a monitor screen so I can see the people downstairs, then I'll have something to feed off. It's a hard job without them." Simon mirrors the manager's emotion with an exaggerated shrug of his own.

"No CCTV, just DJ like it's a party. What's your name again?" the manager shouts over the music, while taking stock of the DJ's silver, side-parted hair.

"Simon."

"Just do it, Simon. Party and come on!"

The manager disappears back into the hallway's darkness and Simon is left staring at the vacuum beyond the ice blue lights of the mixer. Reluctantly, he turns his body and takes his fingers to the back of his record box where the wedding vinyl is quarantined. Playing pop music to an empty room can damage the psyche. Simon pours a little of the cheap house red into a glass and takes a mouthful, sucking the air of the empty library room over his tongue.

Simon picks the chirpy darkness of Michael Jackson from a worn sleeve. He slips the vinyl onto the record deck, drops the stylus into the space between tracks and finds the kick drum with the headphones. He blends the cross rhythms with the vari speed control, flicking and pulling the platter with his fingers. Simon's audio stealth coaxes Michael into the air around the shelves, and the fullness of two records playing simultaneously is absorbed into the record collection of the dead man.

A gaggle of middle-aged ladies are the first to enter the room.

"Rihanna?" comes the first shouted request in a strong Northern Irish accent.

"Rihannon?" a tall blonde at the back shouts, her teeth partly obscured by a smear of dark red lipstick.

"Despacito?" pops from a glum face almost as low as the glow from the decks' needle light.

"Something good?" somebody says as Simon turns his back to pick the next record.

The wedding section is about to be rinsed as the reality of Simon's job strikes home.

"I like you. Will you come to my house in Umbria and play music?" asks a tall lady with jet black hair, her nose sparkling with glitter in the candlelight. "We can pay for the flights," she offers, attempting to seal the deal right there and then.

"Not for me, thanks," responds Simon distantly as he

searches for the dull thud of the kick on the next record he is cueing up in the headphones.

The gaggle of well-to-do ladies pile their expensively collected handbags into a nook by the bookcase.

Simon delivers exactly what they need with a look of suppressed boredom written over his face. The ladies' batteries start to fade as the men arrive. Occasionally they ask Simon to make them drinks and he responds with a look of confusion, while pointing at the black Technics record decks in front of him at waist height. It's 1:30 a.m. and the room is darker than candlelight.

A short and stocky male is in Simon's face offering opinions from rasping pink lips, slippery wet with London dry gin. "This music is awful," he shouts at him over the bar.

"What did you say?" Simon's ears ring too much to pick out his posh voice over the music.

"This crap, what is it?" the posh voice bellows.

"May I ask what you do?" Simon offers a fake smile.

"Me? Well, I'm a fund manager," the banker pronounces proudly.

"If I came to your place of work and called your choices awful how would you react?" Simon raises his voice so the man can hear.

"I'd say I wouldn't like it," the banker replies sheepishly.

"Please, if you could just sit down and behave yourself, sir." Simon points toward one of the empty alcoves at the back of the library bar.

"Can I ask for 'Everything Counts' by Depeche Mode?" says the banker.

Simon nods with a sigh, reaches in his box for the seven-inch and lines it up next. But by then the banker has left the

club and isn't around to see how well the song has cleared the
dance floor. Simon needs a long record to play now; it's time to
take a toilet break. The seven-minute mix of Roberta Gilliam's
"All I Want Is My Baby" gets him to the unisex toilet and back
again. Lately these trips to the bathroom have become a little
too regular for his liking.

A grab bag of tired hits helps him ride the dancers through
to the end of the night. The last track is a reggae re-rub of
Stevie Wonder's "Superstition". The room empties out and an
earth hum spills from the speakers. The dissonant tone blends
awkwardly into the ringing in Simon's ears. He shakes Patryk's
wet hand, says his goodbyes to the rest of the staff holed up on
the first floor counting the night's takings, and heads down to
the street for a ride home.

Outside, the homeless are having a field day with the
drunken members of the club; alcohol has carved the members
a temporary conscience. The swaying figures dressed in haute
couture hand out notes like club flyers in the dull ache of the
Portobello street lights.

Simon's taxi pulls up. He warns the pickled club members
away from the car's back door and gets in. The cab driver
weaves him through the empty streets of Ladbroke Grove,
arriving back at Simon's flat at 3:30 a.m. He dumps his record
boxes in the kitchen, opens up an over-familiar drawer and
rolls a spliff. He smokes half of it out the lounge window.

At 4 a.m. he slips into what's available of the quilt on their
king size bed. Sonia is asleep. He lays his head on the pillow
and tries to forget how little he gets paid for the permanent
ringing that lives inside his head.

2

The Introduction

Simon fell in love with Sonia when he saw her dancing at a house party in Willesden. She moved with night-time magic and her body wrapped around the rhythms of an online edit of Level 42's "Children Say". Her dark green eyes had flecks of orange that sought the light Simon thought had dimmed inside of him. He had decided he wanted to marry her right there and then. Simon believes that the true soul of a person is revealed when they are dancing. The wallpaper in the Willesden cellar was wet with condensation and the 4 am tempos had settled in. It took five dates in various bars, coffee houses and restaurants before the physical seal was broken and another way of being could begin. Sonia was nine years younger and the opposite of Simon: thoughtful where he overthought, connected where he broke ties.

They got married in a Catholic church on the Kensal Green High Road. Simon was concerned there had been a funeral procession down the street just as the guests arrived. Sonia reminded him it was London and that anything you could think of was probably happening somewhere else as well. After eighteen months of marriage, Sonia wasn't ready to have a baby, but nature was sending her messages. She was too practical, worried about money. Again, in this they were opposites — she had married an artist. Her father had kept asking her, who's going to pay for everything?

Simon believed a little too much in fate and pieces of musical magic paying the bills, until the remixes stopped coming in. They made love to a calendar, waiting for the pregnancy tests to indicate a win. It didn't work out. Now their arms reach back to feel the rough brickwork of a bedroom wall closing in on them.

Simon occasionally wonders what happens when you try to make babies when most of a lifetime has passed. Sonia, on the other hand...

"We have a thirty percent increased chance of having a Down syndrome baby. We need to think about these things," she tells him from the sofa in the open-plan lounge, after the 8 o'clock news. Her blonde hair is shining in the light of the reclaimed industrial lamp hanging over her.

"We could get killed in a terrorist attack," Simon replies from his Le Corbusier bentwood chair, which is tucked under the circular dining table near the bay window, overlooking the cars parked in the street beneath them.

Sonia sighs, brow furrowed. "You don't choose to be in a terrorist attack."

"Down syndrome babies are great babies; I know a couple who have one, a beautiful kid," says Simon, while searching Down syndrome on his phone.

"But would you really want one?" Sonia asks.

"I don't know. I've always wanted children and I've been trying to tell you that in lots of different ways. I suppose if it doesn't work out, you can have a puppy farm and I'll have a free pass to smoke weed and stare at the trains from the balcony all day," Simon says, half joking.

14

"You know I'm the one who's had to make all the money recently and I'm not joking. Our bodies are old, things go wrong," Sonia says.

"You're telling me. I've developed a strong urge to sit down for a number one." Simon adds another symptom to his list, which includes a need for long disco edits to get him to the toilet and back when he's working at the Ilithios club.

Sonia looks dead at him. "Something up?"

"I'm just getting lazy." Simon tries to play it down.

"You could be ill," Sonia suggests, sounding exasperated.

"We both know I'm sick." He's not joking.

"Every single one of us is dealing with something, Simon. Only artists think they have a monopoly over it. My sister tried to have a baby with her husband for fifteen years and it didn't work out. We'll be the last remaining members of our families if it stays this way." Sonia hasn't stopped seeking out his blue eyes.

Simon stares at a piece of rice stuck to his old friend the floor as the sound of heavy duty prop planes passes over head. "Has the Queen had another show put on for her today?" he says.

"Probably. I've no idea," says Sonia as Simon stands up to look at the window and search the sky.

He catches two Spitfires and a bigger four-engine plane just before they disappear behind the clouds. Simon had tried to make an Airfix model of a Lancaster as a child, but it got covered in so much glue it had ended up in the loft, out of sight and out of mind.

"The doctor said you should get your sperm count analysed," Sonia continues. "We've had sex religiously for four years now and..."

"You've done well for a Catholic," quips Simon with a wry smile, knowing he shouldn't have said it.

"Have you thought who's going to look after us when we get old? Or what life will feel like as the years drift away, when the only focus is just you and me?" Sonia's voice cracks a little.

"No, I haven't. I thought parenthood was more about giving back what was given." Simon shakes his head and purses his lips. "All of this is a mind melt if you let it get that way."

"It's hard to admit it, but I think we both know a child would give us purpose. We have parents that gave us everything, and now it should be our turn to play," says Sonia, looking past Simon and out of the bay window at the shoots growing from the branches of a London plane tree.

"Wanting something and knowing that it just might not happen is quite a dangerous place to be," Simon replies in a voice close to a whisper.

"We need to start digging into what's wrong with us. With you, with me. Both of us," Sonia says seriously.

"You run marathons three times a year and train for them in between. I can't imagine there could be anything wrong with you physically. You put me to shame anyway."

"Until we get checked out, who knows what lies within?" Sonia replies, touching her tummy.

"Alright, let's get it rolling then. Where do I go for that sperm test you mentioned?" Simon pulls his posture up into line, his lifestyle choices flashing before him.

"The GP will refer you on to a specialist. It's easy."

"I'll organize an appointment then," Simon answers, feeling a sense of helplessness as he smells the remnants of a spliff on his fingers.

"I'm looking into IVF. I've been in contact with the assisted conception unit at Guy's and St Thomas," Sonia says with her left hand touching her temple, cradling her innate sense of responsibility.

"I never thought it would come to this but whatever we have to do. I'll be ready, I promise to not let anything get in the way."

3

Testing, Testing, 1,2,3

Regardless of their desire for a baby, Simon has to take a blood test every three months anyway. Ever since his brain developed a dysfunction the doctor has been prescribing him drugs to keep the internal hounds at bay. The valproic acid in the purple Mepic tablets endanger his liver, and the blood tests are used to evaluate the state of play in his essential organs. Dr Patel is responsible for saving Simon's life. She persuaded him to stick with the drugs after he decided he was better and didn't need to take them anymore. It was only when he almost split with Sonia and their dog refused to be walked by him that the penny dropped. Some things will never pass, and people who take these drugs are always capable of a relapse, especially if they refuse to accept their alternative form of life sentence.

Dr Patel is close to retirement now. She is wrinkled and ashen. Her small arthritic hands pop out from the sleeve of her brown nylon suit as she grips the mouse and scrolls through Simon's medical notes in the local surgery.

"Do you feel ready to have a baby, Simon?" she asks, looking up from the antique personal computer screen shrouded in a brittle off-white plastic.

"Ready? I'm 48 years old. I've never been more ready. My

wife suggested I should come and get my sperm checked, though," he replies with a shift forward and a squeak of his seat.

"I mean in reference to your problem, Mr Radcliffe." Her warm, wise brown eyes search Simon's pale blue eyes. She needs to look right into them and remind him of a few things. "Is it right to bring a child into your world?" she asks softly.

"What do you know about my world?" Simon sounds unconvinced of his own question.

"Well, I'm reading your notes and I can see that it's not long ago that you decided you didn't require your medication. How did that go?" she asks gently, head slightly bowed and her eyes peering over her black reading glasses.

"I know, I know, you were right. I'm dealing with my brain. Everything is under control. I'm more worried about my ears; my ears are my job and they won't stop ringing. That's enough to drive you mad, you know?"

"I can organize a sperm test for you now, Mr Radcliffe. I suggest while we're at it we do as many blood tests as we can," Dr Patel's fingers click away on the old PC keyboard.

"I'm fit and healthy. I play five-a-side once a week. I can barely walk afterwards," Simon replies pointing at his knees.

"Exactly, Mr Radcliffe. I'm going to put you forward for one of our tinnitus groups. They deal with mental health issues as well."

"Where would the group meet?" Simon asks, rubbing at the two-day-old stubble on his square jaw line.

"Over in Wembley. Your attendance will help with the IVF treatment. It means I can give you the green light," she explains, closing out of his records folder with the mouse.

"The green light?" Simon responds quizzically.

"We have to think about what will happen to a child in the future, if the treatment were to be a success," Dr Patel says slowly, carefully.

"You mean you will feel responsible?" Simon coughs the question out.

"Belt and braces, Mr Radcliffe. Your mind is like a blancmange." Dr Patel touches her head to focus the point.

He'd heard this one from her before. "With waxy pieces of string. And the tablets stop my thoughts from getting crossed over. I know. What about these blood tests?"

"I had a son once, Simon, but I lost him. Life is not meant to be easy." Dr Patel's expression is blank, her eyes stare at nothing.

"I'm so sorry for your loss, Dr Patel. I don't know much about these things," replies Simon, shifting in his seat.

"The nurse will do your blood tests now. We will call you if there are any issues. The sperm test will come through soon, hopefully," Dr Patel concludes.

Simon enters a nurse's room down a short corridor in the surgery and a nurse starts preparing to take his blood samples. She lines up eight empty vials and shows Simon to the bed.

"I remember you, Mr Radcliffe. You are the gentleman who sometimes passes out," the nurse says with an understanding South American lilt.

"I'm sorry, nurse. A doctor once shook my drawn blood in a vial without putting the lid on. The blood hit the ceiling and landed all over his white coat. It was like being in a cheap horror film," Simon explains with a wince.

It's the following week and Simon is on his way to Northwick Park Hospital to have his sperm tested. The entrance to the hospital is crowded with pensioners walking canisters of oxygen to the edge of the sliding doors. Simon hurries past the nearly gone and catches an empty lift full of mirrors to the third floor. He signs in at reception. A tall doctor with a pockmarked face and beautiful brown eyes greets him churlishly. He asks Simon to go into the room next door and make love to his sexual memories — and aim the outcome into a transparent collection jar with a white screw top lid.

Like most men, Simon has been practicing sex alone for some time. It all started with The Diary of Anaïs Nin. What led him to pull the erotic paperback from the homemade plywood bookshelf of his parent's dining room was as mysterious as the urge itself. It came out of the blue, rising like a bud seeking the warmth of the sun: ancient, unstoppable and shockingly embarrassing.

Simon's sperm sample results come back a week later and they aren't pretty. There is evidence of sperm but not enough of it to make any difference to an impregnation attempt.

4

The White City

It's a Thursday just after 4:30 p.m. Blue sky is pocked with puffs of cloud shaped like blanched Yorkshire puddings and Simon is DJing in front of the newly reopened BBC building in White City. The DJ stage is set up with steel scaffolding. No one cares what he's playing; it's all about the ambience. It's all for show. The other DJs, of which there are many, are intrigued by his use of vinyl and swarm around his battered record boxes like sarcastic archaeologists.

"Still on it!?" one heavily tattooed USB carrier shouts with mock excitement.

"Hasn't your back gone?" asks another lanky bedroom mixer with a snap back cap and a full flush of Carhartt's recent comeback range.

Simon smiles and raises his eyebrows. He could take out all of these dead stock DJs, but his adrenalin has gone the way of his sperm count. The wind is blowing the awning off the tent that provides rain protection for the racks of amplifiers and compressors. Simon's music blasts meaninglessly over the grassy knoll in front of the stage, bouncing off the sliding doors leading to a hall filled with TV executives who stopped dancing thirty years ago. A strong gust blows the stylus off the record deck across a twelve-inch copy of The Kings of Pressure's "You Know How to Reach Us". Simon scrambles to place the needle back on the record and his phone starts vibrating in his jean pocket.

"Yes, who is this?" he answers curtly, worried about the mix.

"It's the surgery, Mr Radcliffe. It's about your PSA test," explains the male nurse with a Hindi accent.

"What PSA test?"

"It was part of the run of tests your doctor did for you after your last visit to the surgery," the nurse says.

"I see. Just hang on a minute."

Simon tucks the phone under his chin and pulls out a jungle twelve-inch by Firefox & 4-Tree on Philly Blunt Records. He waits for the last snare in the bar and presses stop on the right-hand deck. The snare collapses into a death slur as Simon lets the drum and bass twelve-inch rip the grease from his fingertips and spin on the left deck. The Carhartt-clad DJ, loitering by Simon's box like a discography wasp, pulls a face of excruciating appreciation as the backwards drums and chord stabs fill the warm, early evening air. The last time Simon had played this track he was on a fifty-foot high stage facing twenty thousand festival goers on a hillside in Portugal. The year was 1999, a good one. He had played over two hundred gigs in a tidal wave of self-promotion across the globe that year.

"Are you still there?" Simon shouts into the phone as he turns the monitor down on the Pioneer mixer, just enough to stop the spitting top end of the drum break interfering with the incoming voice on his phone.

"Yes, Mr Radcliffe. It's about your PSA test. It came back very high," the nurse informs him, barely audible.

"That's good. Thanks for letting me know," Simon replies hurriedly with the phone pressed into his neck, leaving his hands free to rifle through his records.

"It would be better if it was low, Mr Radcliffe."

"This is a warning, warning, warning, warning," the lyrics in the breakdown of the Firefox & 4-Tree track echo around the fresh brick of the BBC courtyard.

"Can I ring you back? I'm in the middle of DJing." Simon is looking at the empty grass and the sliding doors. He is the only DJ on the performance platform; the rest of them have disappeared to find the free bar.

"We need to book you in for an MRI scan, Mr Radcliffe. We will be writing to you in due course." The nurse in the surgery concludes the call.

Simon checks his watch. He has twenty minutes more to play, but no one is listening. He grabs the opportunity to play a couple of two-step soul tracks and ends his set with "All The Things We Do When We're Lonely" by Bobby Womack.

In the Uber on the short trip home he looks up the meaning of PSA on his phone. Simon's thumb controls the scroll on his screen as they pass the posters of long gone raves still plastered on the decaying boards lining Scrubs Lane.

"Prostate Specific Antigen," Simon mouths the words softly as the Uber pulls up at the junction of Harrow Road. Feeling car sick, he opts to put the phone down.

5

There's a War Going on Outside

The next morning Simon is woken by a blackbird spitting a warning into the West London ether: three kids got stabbed in Harlesden last night and sixty brand new Volkswagens are riding the overground tracks east. The weight of rolling steel shakes the bricks and a freshly hatched caterpillar drops from the steel railings onto the roof top patio floor. Sonia left for her work as a marketing executive at Four Core Mining an hour ago; now she would be fighting through the crowds of commuters on the streaky brown Bakerloo line. Simon is still asleep under the covers, pinned down by a cloak of medicine that dampen his dark dreams: dreams that sometimes impel him to talk, and even walk, during the night. So far, he hasn't found a source for the evil his mind conjures up when he's sleeping.

Simon knows that Peter Gabriel could be waiting for him in a cardboard mailer downstairs, at the foot of their dark purple front door. His Discogs app had informed him it had been posted out yesterday. Simon's been collecting records to sample from, trying to make a future from a digitally dealt bad hand.

The vibration from a passing goods train wakes Simon from his slumber. After putting on a dressing gown, he heads downstairs to gather the post, his arms shining bright courtesy of his studio tan. The record mailer is there, with a copy of Quantize Magazine strapped to it with a Post Office rubber band. He fills the kettle and turns it on with a click. It will take an hour before his liver can flush the prescription drugs out of his system. He sits at the table and opens the post in the grey morning light of the lounge bay window.

Slipping the vinyl out of the mailer, he sees Gabriel's melting face staring up at him. He thumbs through the magazine. Last Physical Edition! the Quantize cover exclaims. The publishers are moving the operation online and giving away an app that corrects the timing of "any sounds played into your phone". Simon inputs the code and a Bakelite metronome fades into a box on the screen.

He opens a music royalty statement and the paper cuts his finger. Pretty pennies sieved from all over the world add up to £19.44. He vows to spend it on a new pack of vitamins to help improve the viability of his sperm.

The second letter is from the National Happy Service, a body dedicated to the promotion of the healthy mind; the same Happy Service that prescribed Simon the chemicals to balance his mood swings. The Mepic he takes is normally given to people who suffer from epilepsy; it also helps people stitch their thoughts back together, or so his doctor had told him.

Simon takes the tiny Opalune pills in the evening, hoping to ward off the terror that sometimes visits in the night. He often wakes up in different rooms in the house and sleep talks like an actor in the cast of a 1950s Pinewood Studios film. The Opalune tablets taste bitter, just like the memories they suppress. In his dreams he is often flying and the black earth below him burns out of control.

The Happy Service wants him to go one step further than

medication alone. Just as his GP had predicted, Simon must also attend a weekly counselling session called Rings and Things. The sessions occur every Wednesday in a portacabin next to a roundabout by an industrial park on the outskirts of Wembley. If he doesn't attend the allotted number of Rings and Things sessions, Simon and Sonia's access to IVF could be denied.

6

On Our Way to Wembley

It's 10 o'clock in the morning. Simon sits at the front of an empty 187 bus snaking its way through the slim streets of Harlesden. The hiss of pneumatic doors welcomes the occasional passenger as the diesel fumes cast their invisible spells.

Alighting on the Park Royal industrial estate, Simon crosses the busy road and climbs up some clanking metal steps to the door of a large portacabin, painted in battleship grey. Inside the mobile room, a semi-circle of cheap plastic chairs stab their rusty legs into the linoleum.

A tall, dark-haired lady called Liz, dressed in an apple green jumper, is getting ready for the first session of the day. She works part time for the Happy Service. Technically she's only a trainee, she explains. Earning flying hours, helping out while trying to find her own way.

Sat on the chairs in front of her are five men cast out like gnarled wood dumped on the high tide line. Liz begins the session by asking each of the men to introduce themselves. A man called Robert sits with his arms folded tight over his taught, distended stomach. He's a former pub landlord with dark curly hair, streaked with silver. Robert's ears went funny

28

after listening to a heavy rock band cover "Doctor Doctor" by the Thompson Twins during a pub lock-in. Anger is carved into his face like someone took a switchblade to a lump of pork crackling. Tony is sat next to Robert on a red chair. He's a big man, bald and muscular with tanned skin. Tony works as a builder and likes to dance all night to high-energy disco. He suffers from a constant whistling noise and white finger from repetitive use of pneumatic drills. Andy, in the blue chair, is pasty-faced and skinny with pointed features and a rave ponytail. He is the father of several children with various women. He's not sure how he damaged his hearing, but it comes in useful to pretend he is deaf when arguing with his babies' mothers. Rupert sits in the yellow chair. He has short, un-styled brown hair, is plump and sexlessly cuddly. He works as an online marketing expert, barks like a dog and suffers from Tourette's syndrome. They think his hearing problem is, possibly, self-inflicted. Finally, on the last grey chair is Wilf, a former dockworker. Half Yorkshire, half African, Wilf's right ear was damaged by the clank of heavy iron; he's strong, hard and not for turning.

Simon takes his seat after a brief round of head nods.

"So, gentlemen," says Liz, getting the ball rolling. "Thank you so much for coming to today's Rings and Things. This course is devised to help you adapt to your hearing problems and deal with the kind of mental health issues that we can all encounter, from day to day."

"Or all day, every day," adds Andy, itching the flaky skin off his elbow.

"We are here to make a difference together, Andy. It really does take a lot of collective effort for us all to share and open up," Liz adds. Lifting her open palm away from her side she gathers the men's eyes up to the board. On the board various words are spelled out in badly drawn boxes:

Understanding
Respect
Community
Acceptance
Volume
Repetition
Tuning out
The Past
Acceptance
Anger
Belonging
Closure

Liz continues: "So, can we all have a look at the board? Take in some of the issues that could affect us in relation to how we feel," she says, pausing and sharing her soft, almond-brown eyes with the room, "about life and disability."

Robert's hand flies up.

"Yes, Robert," says Liz.

"There's a dick on the board." Robert points to the bottom of the blackboard with a grotesque smirk.

Liz quickly wipes the crudely drawn image away.

"There's some dicks in this room," mumbles Andy.

"OK, guys," says Liz. "We talked a bit about belonging last week. Can anyone remember what the various forms of belonging are?"

"Family," Wilf replies.

"Yes, family is a good one, Wilf. Thank you for that."

"What happens if you hate your family?" offers Robert.

"I'm a hammer 'til I die," Tony says under his breath.

"OK, Robert," says Liz. "Well, of course our relationship with family is very important in how we shape our lives and —" Liz pauses as the handle of the portacabin door squeaks and moves down, "... and our worlds," she finishes, putting her palms together like a globe.

The door swings open and a paper plane with a butterfly drawn on its wings flies on a cold breeze and rests beneath Simon's chair.

"Ah, for God's sake. Kids taking the piss. Hope you locked that moped up, Tony," mumbles Robert, standing up to shut the door.

But a body appears in the doorway, growing in height as it traverses the steps. Soon very broad shoulders fill the doorframe and Robert retreats to his chair.

"Hello, there," says Liz as the middle-aged men look on like punched rabbits with hangovers.

"Hi," replies a tall man, his voice soft and deep.

"Please, come in and take a seat." Liz offers him a chair.

"I am Tobias," the man replies, bowing as though he were Japanese.

Liz picks up her attendance sheet and scans for indication of a new arrival.

Tobias is at least six-foot-three. He wears a long, white lab coat. Piercing the lapel is a two-centimetre gold badge: a caterpillar with two purple stones for eyes. Around his neck he wears a golden tinted stethoscope. His face is square-jawed and strong. A refined, thin nose cuts the air in front of him. His studied eyes are slate grey, and his limbs are lean and long.

31

"Sorry, I don't seem to have another person down for the session today," Liz says, showing him to a spare chair placed against the wall. "But please feel free to join us. Time is moving on."

"It is, isn't it?" Tobias replies as he picks the plastic chair up, glides across the floor in his grey Birkenstock sandals, and places the chair next to Simon, who can't help but stare at his elegant bony hands.

Liz starts the session with some "Engaging Questions", but Simon is too distracted by the late arrival to pay attention. The room seems to be talking about diet, mental health and the problems associated with being professionally angry. Robert's increasingly desperate story about his failed pub pulls Simon's attention from Tobias's bony hands and he is back in the room.

"More people are drinking at home now and what was I going to do about that? I couldn't get a reduction from the breweries. Bang, bosh, the pubs gone bust and I'm sat at home with all the barrels," Robert moans.

"If you can't beat 'em, join 'em!" pipes up Tony.

"Thank you for sharing with us, Robert." Liz pulls her clasped hands in to her chest and cocks her head to the side.

"Can you expand on that? Tell us how that made you feel?"

"When people stopped drinking in my pub, it gave me anxiety. I got absentminded and one day I fed the dog some tinned food that was out of date," Robert continues angrily.

"I can see that you were upset that your business was going through hard times," interjects Liz, "but did you see any difference in your mental state between when you drank alcohol, and when you didn't?"

"I started drinking heavily when the dog died of botulism and people stopped drinking in my pub."

32

"It was the drink that drove him to the drink," observes Wilf, to a round of titters.

"Gentlemen, if you do drink, please read the Happy Service guidelines. They really are there to help," says Liz.

"You're another one that's part of the problem," mumbles Robert.

"You can only help people who actually want help, surely," Simon says, reaching for sense.

"Interesting point, Simon. Now, moving on, does anybody know the impact that sugar has on the body?" Liz asks with a tired smile.

A collective sigh meets her attempts to retell exhausted stories. The final half-hour of the session involves an argument over the price of courgettes and the correct way to make baba ghanoush. Robert is convinced that baba ghanoush was a left back for Tottenham Hotspur and spends ten minutes on his phone trying to prove it. No one cares. Tobias watches them all with a slightly concerned look. He turns to Simon and a warm smile creeps across his face. All the talk of food sees Robert and Andy head straight for the kebab shop when the session ends.

Simon wasn't expecting much from the session; it had gone about as well as he had expected it to go. He is waiting for the bus home, looking down at his glowing phone and scrolling through while sitting on the steel seats. He clicks on an article linking Euro rave with mad cow disease and a familiar pair of sandals shift into his peripheral vision.

"Maybe we are going the same way, Simon?" Tobias asks in a softly accented tone that Simon is unable to place.

"Hi. It's Tobias, yes? Where are you off to then?"

"Not sure. Might just let the evening unfold naturally," Tobies replies with a gentle shrug and a nod.

"I get the 187. About a ten-minute wait," Simon replies with a hint of boredom.

"The 187 is coming in ten minutes, then another in eleven minutes, then another will be here in thirteen," remarks Tobias.

"It's a modern way of proving a rather old point," Simon remarks, looking up at the digital display attached to the plastic bus stop ceiling.

"If you don't mind me asking, how old are your shoes?" asks Tobias politely. Simon looks down at his almost box fresh but completely out of fashion skate shoes.

"They're about fifteen years old. I haven't worn them much. They were given to me," Simon replies with a hint of distaste.

"People gave you free shoes? Were you some kind of big shot back then?" Tobias raises one of his eyebrows and the gold plating on his stethoscope catches the light.

"Yeah, it's a long story." Simon groans.

"I see. Do you want to tell me more?" Tobias is standing up, his head almost touching the display of arrival times.

"Only if you tell me why you have those sandals," Simon points at the grey Birkenstocks covering Tobias's naturally tanned feet.

"OK, you go first." Tobias smiles and Simon takes in a deep breath.

"Once upon a time, marketing people thought it was a good idea to give me free things so that if somebody saw me wearing them, they might want to buy them," explains Simon.

"That sounds a little farfetched," Tobias replies, his unplaceable Northern European accent more evident in the pronunciation of his last two words.

"I agree, the chances of someone buying such ugly skate shoes is, as you say, pretty ridiculous," Simon adds grumpily.

"They are just like children's shoes, aren't they? So how did we get here?" says Tobias.

"I remixed pop stars back in the day, gave them some flavour from the underground, and now it seems I'm back down there to stay," says Simon as a bus appears a hundred yards down the road from them.

The 98 bus pulls up and a gaggle of plastic bag-gripping pensioners shuffle in a line to get on to the boxy red bus.

"OK, this is me. See you then," Simon aims his goodbye at Tobias, hoping to escape the strange line of questioning.

"No, this is my bus too," Tobias moves with him to the bus door.

"Oh, Christ," Simon mumbles under his breath before heading upstairs to see more sky from the window. Tobias follows, swinging his lithe body into position, big hands gripping the metal poles. He lands next to Simon on the paint-splattered seat.

"Your clothes are old-fashioned too, aren't they, Simon?" he whispers.

"You're a bit of a snob, Tobias," Simon says, trying to laugh it off.

"Oh, dear, dear me, Simon. You really shouldn't push someone away who is trying to help now, should you?" Tobias offers on the edge of condescension.

"Help? If your definition of helping someone is to critique their clothes, then you really must have had an unusual upbringing."

"I am only reporting on my observation of your appearance,

yet you are questioning my origins?" Tobias replies, sounding a little hurt.

"Jesus, you're a wind up." Simon stares at the pollution-stained shopfronts of the Willesden high street passing slowly in the window.

A few seconds of uncomfortable silence conspires to feel like a minute.

"Look, Simon. I can see you are a frustrated man. I can also see you are struggling." Simon glares out the window as Tobias continues. "But things have been changing. The soil is being turned over and the farmer has need of a new harvest. Special people can get buried, covered over, and it's not all their fault." Tobias sighs as he concludes with a sharp intake of breath.

"Huh... and?" Simon shrugs his shoulders, bemused.

"You need money to feel like a man, don't you, Simon?" Tobias looks him in the eye, holding his gaze.

"No, I don't," replies Simon haughtily.

"I know that you do," Tobias says.

"Everyone is always in need of money, especially the rich," Simon sneers.

"Not as much as you and your wife need money right now. I would like to help. Really." The two amethysts on his gold lapel pin glow as Tobias turns his palms out in a show of honesty.

A familiar church spire catches Simon's eye; it's a signal that the journey is nearly over. Getting off the bus two stops early will keep this peculiar, well-mannered stranger from knowing where he lives. Simon delivers a quick "bye" aimed at Tobias's chest and clambers down the stairs to exit the bus's hissing double doors. He marches down the jagged pavement, which has been broken into random triangles by tree roots, arriving at his flat still agitated by the exchange with Tobias. Simon has always felt suspicious toward people who try to offer financial advice, even more so, men who wear any kind of jewellery. He picks his phone up and texts the weed man.

Half an hour later Simon meets his dealer in the Dead Dog. The short Hungarian has an impish smile. The pub is almost empty. A table at the back is filled with tipsy mums ignoring their babies.

Simon orders two of the cheapest drinks available on the menu and sits himself down next to the weed man, who is dressed in a nylon flight jacket and ripped jeans. The pair start a stilted conversation while, under the table, their hands exchange £20 for a bag of hydroponic herb. Thirty seconds later they exit the Dead Dog, leaving two full diet cokes fizzing away untouched.

Back at the flat Simon takes off his coat like a man with an incurable fever, his flailing arm knocking a container of folic acid tablets onto the kitchen floor. Simon ignores the mess. He has to get a joint rolled up fast. The meeting with Tobias has left him on edge and a new beat is already rattling around his mind in response. Music has always been Simon's coping mechanism and time gets squashed when you're prone to getting lost in music: seconds become minutes and minutes become more than just time.

With a Rizla wrap of borrowed inspiration tucked behind his ear, he heads to the back of the flat where a sash window overlooks the train tracks. Climbing onto the lead roof he searches for a playlist on his phone, rests his back on the wall and sparks up the joint. The Rizla paper crackles. Unfinished demos dance around in his brain as he inhales the dirty combination. His demos are his babies and Simon has more of them than he needs or would care to mention. With his mind tainted by the smoke fused into the bloodstream, he climbs down from the roof and heads to the room where the audio alchemy occurs.

Simon's studio is small and dusty with a thick Turkish rug covering almost all the cream nylon carpet it lies upon. The walls are lined with shelving packed tight with records; the shelves are screwed against the wall in case the content falls in on him, like his business did ten years before. The mid-eighties drum machines sit on his orange Ikea desks like artefacts of the cold war. An Akai MPC 60 with thick grey rubbery buttons, a boxy EMU SP1200 that gets too hot, and an ESI32 sampler which Simon uses for hoovering up large chunks of other people's records into his own creations. Alchemy addiction, doing it for the music is the spin: seventies samples, eighties memories and the nineties, when Simon rode the music business tiger, and created a remix agency that dragged him into the cheap bin.

He pulls the albums out by their fraying spines and slides the vinyl out, catching the Shellac blade in the palm of his hand, holding it up to the light by the tips of his fingers. Musical breakdowns reflect at different angles, a road map making trips around the vinyl, evidence that samples may lay within.

Drop the bomb! reads the tagline on a bootleg album with a warthog's face snarling on the cover. All this loud music has left Simon's ears with an artillery ring. But he can't turn away from the breach or move his heart from the flame.

He reaches for the Peter Gabriel album and pulls the disk from the inner sleeve with the tips of his fingers. The hole finds the spindle and the shining black disk drops down to the slipmat. With a casual tap of the decks' start button, the record begins to spin, the needle drops, and the speakers crackle. The stylus glides through the artist's feelings etched into the grooves.

The melancholy piano of Peter Gabriel's "Family Snapshot" spills out into the dimly lit room. Simon's ready to borrow time and make the past begin. Copy, chop, slice and discard, Gabriel's face stares back, melting and dripping down the sleeve. Simon's face is focused, in search of the jigsaw piece to make the track sing. He's basking in the warmth of creation, swimming in possibilities laden with sample sin. Time is lost to diggers when they learn to sacrifice everything.

Simon pauses and looks at the studio clock. Sonia will be back home soon. He exits the studio's musty electronic heat, scrubs the evidence of smoke from his fingers in the bathroom sink, and brushes his teeth like he was going on a first date. Sometimes Simon finds it hard to look in the mirror, at least the hair loss on his crown is hidden from view but there's still the bags that hang below the baggage stored within.

The sound of Sonia's key in the front door has him practicing a look of innocence. She enters the kitchen looking shattered, worn to the quick by the work commute and her recent marathon training regime. The clock upstairs runs thirty minutes fast; the clock in the studio is an hour late. Simon gives her a slightly embarrassed hug, his fresh minty breath aimed away. She reaches for the folic acid tablets, shaking them out of the container onto the kitchen counter.

"Oh, there's some hair on these tablets. That's a bit strange."

"It must be from the dog," says Simon.

"The dog died a year ago, honey," she says.

"I know," he says, trapped by his own stupidity.

39

"Have you been taking your Vitamin D? It's supposed to be great for immunity and general health," she says.

Simon rocks from side to side, trying to hide his discomfort. "Not today. I've been outside a lot, stretching the old legs, working Wednesday night's football stiffness away."

"Your eyes look a bit red, darling. Was it windy?" Sonia's expression sharpens a little.

"Yes," says Simon, standing off balance, still running on a quarter tank of THC.

"There's a letter here for you." Sonia picks it up and waves it at him.

Simon takes the letter and opens it. The sight of a Happy Service address sets his eyes away.

"What does it say?" asks Sonia.

"I've got a date for an MRI scan," he replies, his face looking a whiter shade of pale.

7

The Techno Machine

Simon fills out the arrival forms in the waiting room of Charing Cross Hospital's MRI department. The room is stuffy, the ceiling inlayed with two rows of strip lights. Two worried-looking men are sat as far away from each other as possible, filling out their consent forms. Simon hands his completed form to a dangerously thin female nurse with a care-worn face, dressed in a white starched uniform. She checks it over, running her pen up and down the ticks on the page: no pacemaker, no stents, no metal plates. Simon has ticked through them all. She leads him to a row of lockers next to three changing rooms that face the waiting area.

"Take all your clothes off and put this on," says the nurse. "The slit needs to be at the back. Call me if you need help."

The nurse hands Simon a knee-length cotton gown; a blue pattern covers the material. The inside of it feels cheap and rough to the touch. Safety pins hang from the opening at the back of the gown; the ties have snapped with overuse. Simon takes off his clothes and bundles them into a pile on the bench in the changing room. He lifts the gown onto his shoulders and ties the thin collar at the back. Picking up his jumbled garments, he sidles out of the changing room with his backside glowing blueish-white in the ward's strip lights. Simon bends down, forces his clothes into the bottom locker and wraps the key strap around his wrist.

Through the doors, the machine is working overtime, sounding like punching pistons or a child's attempts to recreate the sound of anti-aircraft fire when flying balsa wood planes across back gardens, through lounges and bedrooms.

"We have to inject you with a dye and a relaxant. Is that OK, Mr Radcliffe?" the young assistant specialist with blonde wavy hair and glowing white teeth asks gently.

"Is it essential?" Simon replies with a ropey swallow.

"If we want the results to be accurate, yes, it's important." The assistant rubs his hands together in haste; he must have a lot of patients to scan in the next eight hours.

"I must warn you that I might pass out if it's a needle," Simon says, with both hands gripping the chair.

"Don't worry, Simon. It's a cannula," the assistant says, smiling.

"Can you show it to me?" Simon asks, his lip trembling.

"If that will help you, of course I can." The specialist pulls a cannula wrapped in sterile packaging from the trolley alongside them and shows it to Simon in the palm of his hand.

Simon balks. "It looks like the end of a garden hose."

"We can distract you, Simon. Don't worry." The assistant claps his hands together.

Simon starts to see stars swirling in his peripheral vision and his mind invents a smell that doesn't exist. "I'm going to faint: catch me," he blurts out weakly.

"You're already in a seat, Simon. Just lean back." The assistant places his hand on Simon's shoulder.

Simon comes around in the chair a minute later and finds he's been wheeled into another white room. In front of him is a thick plastic tunnel with a sliding bed aimed into its cavernous core. Banks of computers are linked to the machine with white and green-coloured cables.

"The straps on the bed, what are they for?" Simon asks, his voice quivering.

"We need to keep you still, so the machine can take a clear image," the assistant informs him, flicking at the bubbles trapped in a freshly filled syringe.

"Will it hurt?"

"It will be noisy, that's all. We have headphones to reduce the sound," the specialist explains.

"What is the machine going to do to me?" Simon asks breathlessly.

"It will flip every hydrogen molecule in your body to magnetic north," the assistant tells him proudly.

"Like a compass?" Simon sounds unconvinced.

"Like a magnet, which is why we asked in the questionnaire if you had any metal objects in your body."

"What would happen if I did?" Simon's eyebrows are up to his hairline.

"This machine can throw a wheelchair across a room," the assistant remarks in a low, almost threatening, tone.

"Will it bleach my teeth?"

"No. Please, Simon, climb in." The assistant has crossed from bedside manner into technical mode. Simon climbs onto the sliding bed and they strap him in.

The specialist places a set of noise-cancelling headphones over his ears and puts a grey plastic balloon with a button into his right palm.

"Hold this. Squeeze the button if you feel uncomfortable and we'll stop," the assistant whispers into his ear.

"Uncomfortable? What should I be looking for?" Simon replies anxiously.

"Claustrophobia," comes the assistant's nonchalant reply.

"Why did you say that?" Simon sounds disgusted.

"Because you asked, Mr Radcliffe."

"What about my fillings? I've got a soldering club's worth of seventies metalwork in here," Simon explains, pointing into his mouth.

"Copper and Mercury are not magnetic enough to cause any problems."

The assistant squeezes the liquid mixture into the injection port of the cannula. A subtle whisper of cold creeps up Simon's arm, the Buscopan formula slips into his muscles, and the contrast dye slides through his veins on a journey to mark out every corner of his body. A chemical cartographer, plotting shapes with its liquid pen.

The specialist takes hold of the bed next to Simon's feet and gently pushes him into the gaping hole. The magnetic symphony begins.

Thack, gick, tizz, erp, arp, Aaaaaaaaa.

Thirty minutes of computer noise spits away inside the plastic tube. Simon is trapped in a techno tunnel where the sound of electromagnets decide if he is going to die or live.

He clings on to the rescue squeeze ball and moves his thumb softly against the button until the room falls quiet. The doctor grabs the foot of the bed and slides him out of the hole in the machine in one swift movement. The change of light is blinding. Simon squeezes his eyes shut for ten seconds and feels a presence appear next to him.

44

"How was that then?" the specialist asks Simon, as she helps him sit up and pull his legs round.

"The music was terrible, and the crowd weren't much better either."

The specialist and the assistant don't respond because they're already focussed on the next patient who has to be racked up on the MRI machine.

Outside the hospital Simon stumbles down the high street as the Buscopan interacts with the Mepic in his blood stream. His blancmange wobbles in time with his steps; he feels useless. Arriving at the Hammersmith tube station he sits down on an empty train with an exaggerated slump. The train departs. He gets off one stop too early and has to get back on the next train. There's a sense of calm in his chemically induced stupidity.

When Simon gets back to the flat, Sonia is making a cup of tea in their open-plan kitchen. She welcomes him with a kiss and waits for the rumble of the kettle to finish boiling.

"How did that go?"

"It was a bit like a DJ gig I did in Oakland when all the kids were laid out in sleeping bags on ketamine and Andrew Weatherall played techno to them through the gaps in their zips," Simon replies, slurring slightly.

"Do you feel OK?" she asks, peering into his glassy, disorientated eyes.

"I feel righteously pathetic," Simon musters.

"I'm so sorry for you, honey. I really am. But, the thing is, Guys and Thomas have been in touch and we've been accepted for two free rounds of ICSI," Sonia says, delivering the IVF news with a ruffle of excitement.

Simon squints. "ICSI? It sounds like a disease that rabbits might catch."

"It's a technique where the sperm is injected directly into the egg," Sonia explains with gleeful seriousness.

"But I'm not that lazy. I can, we can, you know," Simon says, his voice tailing off into a dull mumble.

"It's our best chance of success," Sonia states adamantly.

"Are two goes of ICSI enough for us to get pregnant then?"

"Some couples do it ten times and nothing happens."

"Christ, we better get started then."

"We already have. They've sent the drugs to inject and sniff." Sonia points to a white paper bag on the kitchen counter.

"I think I might pass out with the needles."

"Not everything is about you, Simon."

"I know, or at least I hope it doesn't turn out to be," he replies, with the echo of the MRI machine pinging in the shadows of his tinnitus-riddled ears.

For three weeks, Sonia prepares her body. She injects Buserelin into her stomach in the bathroom away from Simon's cowardly view. On the closed lid of the toilet she sits and injects Gonal-F and Menopur into the top of her athletic thighs. The drugs will plump her eggs up like round pillows of propensity. Simon feels faint just thinking about it and hides in the lounge, watching the siege of Leningrad play out on the Yesterday channel.

They attend a hospital appointment to assess the follicular growth; it looks positive and a trigger injection is advised. Within thirty-six hours, five of Sonia's eggs have been plucked out under sedation. Whatever moving sperm the specialist could find in Simon's sample have been individually injected;

it comes as a shock to him that they have managed to find five. Two of the eggs start developing and become the very smallest version of a human. Sonia is prepared with Gestone injections and the blastocysts are placed delicately against the womb wall. When it's over they walk out of the hospital together, lurid flashes of the sun splashing on their faces and across the blue tinted glass of the Shard. They hold hands, knowing they've just strapped into an un-named roller coaster.

8

Second-hand Pram

Simon is on his knees in the charity shop looking through records again. This spot can throw up the odd sample if you choose to visit regularly. The smell of the past mixed with damp biscuits drifts up from the charity shop floor. Irish Frank, the local jazz dancer, died in his bed last month — too much cubed cheese and Guinness. Frank's daughter brought his cherished vinyl collection down to the charity shop and Simon saw her dropping them off from the café over the road. The deceased's daughter was still at the counter when Simon arrived, panting like a sweaty sample rat thundering up a sax baritone.

"I'm sorry for your loss," Simon says while waiting politely for her to leave.

Irish Frank married a Brazilian lady; it didn't last long but the music stuck to him like a hot Twix in a bag full of stickle bricks.

"Reminds me of the sex," he used to say to Bossa Nova enthusiasts in the bars of Soho. Now Frank's prized collection of Brazilian imports is slumped at an angle, propped up against the plastic, tracked wheels of a toy-armoured vehicle at the back of the shop. A Flora Purim album at the front of the pile is still damp with the tears of Frank's daughter. She couldn't keep herself together when she carried them to the shop to let the records go.

Simon paid £8 for the soundtrack to Frank's sex life. The vinyl is too heavy for the second-hand Tesco bags they were delivered in. Behind the till, a blonde Polish assistant with stark blue eye shadow points to a chrome and black pram parked next to the entrance. Simon buys it for a tenner and loads the vinyl. Pushing it back to the flat, the faces of the Brazilian musicians on the record sleeves stare up at him, bouncing along with the bumps in the path. He loads the vinyl into his studio at the back of the flat and carries the pram up the stairs with a few huffs and puffs.

Sonia returns from her run after work and gets a little emotional when she sees the pram, its sparkling chrome trim catching the sun in the lounge window.

"That's so thoughtful," she says, her gentle Northumbrian accent caressing the air in the room.

"It's a bit retro though, don't you think?" Simon fusses with the material lining the inside.

"It's perfect. I like the penguin motif. It reminds me of one of my sister Joanna's toys. When I think of what she went through trying to get pregnant, part of this makes me feel sort of guilty and, well, a bit scared." Sonia grabs the handle and pushes the pram to and fro.

"You shouldn't feel that way."

"I know but I can't help it. I was the only one she shared the experience with other than her husband John.

Simon crouches down to take in the logo and notices how much his hair is turning grey in the prams reflective finish. "I guess it's just a brand," he says. "Penguin Prams has a ring to it." He cups his hand over Sonia's tummy and pulls her in.

"How long do we have to wait?" he asks her with a squeeze of her hips.

"We can use the home pregnancy test in the next few days," she says.

Simon's eyes shift. "I hope I haven't gone and jinxed it."

"Jinxed what?" she asks as the pram freewheels two feet across the worn lounge carpet.

"Don't worry, honey. Forget it." He banishes his thoughts behind a less than convincing smile.

"There's another letter for you on the counter by the fridge," Sonia says, pointing over to the bread bin.

Simon opens the letter while biting into an apple. He stops chewing when he reads the word: biopsy.

9

Operation Biopsy

Simon is on the front seats of the top deck of a 190 bus. He's on his way from Hammersmith tube to Charing Cross Hospital. Another 190 is ahead; Simon imagines there is a 190 behind. He turns to check. Yes, it's a London special: a convoy of the same number. The bus behind is empty and the bus in front has one broad-shouldered figure sat on the top deck. Simon is sure it's someone he knows. The three 190 buses pull up to the hospital stop. Simon alights and waits to see who gets off the bus in front before moving.

The broad figure in a lab coat gets off; Simon exits the path into the hedges covering the entrance to the hospital and walks in time with the figure, keeping out of sight a few metres back. Simon stops on the grass and waits for the figure to turn side on at the entrance path. Simon feels sick flanking another human like this, stalking them like prey. He's sure it's Tobias. But the figure turns to reveal a pale complexion, a shorter nose. It's not him and the thought dissolves, leaving him to worry about the day ahead.

The smell of the hospital hits him as he enters the rotating doors. Simon takes the lift to arrive at the pre-op ward on the fourth floor. He introduces himself to three nurses who are hunkered down on wheeled seats, tucked behind a plastic veneer desk. They seem especially friendly, almost flirtatious. Then he remembers: it takes special people to steer the unlucky to their deaths. But he's not really dying, or could it be that everyone is dying, all the time? He decides both are equally true and plays with the thought as the nurse gives him a plain white plastic bag to put his clothes in.

She leads him over to his designated bed. In the next bed a stout, black, middle-aged man is laid out unconscious. In front of him another black man sits up in his bed awake and fully clothed. Next to him a twenty-stone white kid is reading Time Out magazine, a bulbous red growth protruding from his head. Simon starts to undress as a plump blonde nurse, dressed in light blue, pulls the green curtain around his bed. The man next to him starts to come around from what must have been a heavy dose of anaesthetic.

"Lovely day for it," Simon offers in a flight of nervous energy. The room responds with smiles and grunts of genial agreement.

The formerly knocked out man comes back to life. "Glad that's all over," he says dozily. "The wife will be in to get me soon." He's upright now and starting to pack his bag.

"What have you had done?" Simon asks.

"Prostate biopsy," the man replies.

"I'm in for one of those too," says Simon nervously.

"Same here," comes the reply in a Jamaican accent from the bed directly opposite.

"This," replies the big kid pointing at the growth screaming in red at the top of his forehead.

"Did you choose to be put under then?" Simon asks the man who was unconscious when he arrived.

"Yes, that's why my wife's picking me up. You can't drive after this kind of operation."

"I'm scared," blurts out Simon as the Jamaican watches on closely. "My wife answered the phone when the doctor couldn't get through to me. I had my music on too loud. Turns out she chose for me to have the procedure without anaesthetic," Simon explains at a hundred miles an hour.

"Had you fallen out with her?" asks the post-op man.

"No, it was just a misunderstanding at their end. What's the operation like then?" Simon asks squinting his eyes with intent.

"I don't know, man, they knocked me out," the man, lucky enough to be leaving, answers with a straight bat.

"Lord 'ave mercy," bellows the Jamaican, overcome with nerves.

"Are you getting a prostate operation too?" asks Simon.

"Yes, man," the Jamaican replies.

"Are you getting knocked out or taking it on the chin? "

"Same, on de chin."

"Good, God. What the hell are they going to do to us?" Simon asks with a whimpering gurn.

"Think of something else. You said you like your music loud," the Jamaican says, coming to the rescue.

"I love nineties dancehall. Do you know Cutty Ranks?" Simon's eyes brighten with the memory.

"Know him? I used to spar with him back a yard," the Jamaican replies triumphantly.

"Dibby dibby DJ," starts Simon.

"Know me a death, know me a death," finishes his hospital friend, and they continue in tight vocal unison, driven by the spectre of the unknown.

"Nuff of them a worry, nuff of them a worry, some of dem a fret," Simon chants, pointing at the Jamaican in time with the vocal cadence.

A tall, slim doctor wearing a green facemask and a hair net enters the room and consults his papers. The conversation and singing abruptly end.

"Mr. Radcliffe?" says the doctor.

Before Simon knows it, he is bidding goodbye to his dancehall buddy and chatting fear-addled nonsense to the doctor, who wheels him down the brightly lit corridor at a steady pace. They pass by the desk with the three nurses he thought fancied him and enters a room that looks like the control room of a spaceship. Chic's "I Want Your Love" is playing in the operation theatre. Studio 54, welcome to the butcher shop.

The bed is parked into a metallic dock where another doctor, wearing blue scrubs, is typing details into the computer. A myriad of triffid-like lights beam down on flexible stalks. Before Simon can even muster a dry-mouthed word, the doctor has put his legs into stirrups; now his bare bottom is aimed at two ladies in green hair nets at the back, who are moving a row of glistening medical weapons into an order of battle.

"This may feel strange," a surgeon explains. "And it might hurt a little. We're going to numb the area so there's less chance of pain while we extract the samples."

"My wife picked up the phone and agreed to this procedure without general anaesthetic, you know," says Simon.

The doctor injects the first dose; it feels like a trickle of ice water has been poured into the centre of Simon's hips. The doctor continues. He's onto the fourth injection before he answers.

"I see. Did you have an argument the night before?" the doctor says, his mahogany brown eyes racked with lifesaving concentration.

"No," Simon replies with a gasp as another injection finds its way into the middle of him.

"Maybe she just wants you to grow through the experience," the surgeon muses. "We'll let this take effect for a few minutes, Simon. Then we'll begin the biopsy. I don't have a lot to aim for so I'm going to fire eighty rods in. If it hurts, I can stop and inject you with more local anaesthetic, OK?"

"What's eighty rods between friends?" Simon lifts his lip like a cheap Elvis impersonator.

A click is followed by the schtoof sound of the compressed air as the biopsy gun fires the first sample rod into the middle of Simon's lower torso. For a moment he sees himself as a man gifted the experience of childbirth, flinching in pain, strapped in stirrups with everyone in the room focused on his body.

10

Untermeyer

Sixteen days later, Simon watches as Sonia sits on the side of the bath and peels the wrapper from a home pregnancy kit. She lifts the ivory lid of the toilet, sits down and takes the test. When she stands up Simon puts his arms around her and they cling on to each other like two penguins on an ice cliff, their breaths held in unison. They stare at the plastic window in the middle of the pen, waiting for an indication of life. The test line fades in and a line of Etch a Sketch grey delivers the news: it's the wrong side of the pregnancy marker.

Sonia's body has provided no sign of the chemicals that would show a baby has started growing inside of her.

She grits her teeth as Simon's phone rings brightly in the tight reverb of the tiled bathroom. It's the hospital and the doctor's secretary would like Simon to come into his office first thing tomorrow, preferably with Sonia.

Simon takes the pregnancy test pen from the side of the sink and gives it a shake. He pushes his thumb against the screen in an attempt to push the grey line up to where they both wanted it to be. He looks in the mirror and presses the bin's peddle with his foot. The lid squeaks as he drops the negative test into the lining of the bin, and it lands with the rustle of plastic.

Sonia retreats to the lounge and Simon senses she is filled with steely determination. Simon looks over her shoulder as she opens her laptop with hurried force and writes a short email explaining she can't come in to work tomorrow.

The following day the couple journey by tube in silence and arrive at the urology department of Charing Cross Hospital for Simon's 10 a.m. appointment. The waiting room on the third floor is filled with aged males.

A doctor eventually appears from his office and introduces himself as Dr Untermeyer. He's dressed in a white shirt tucked neatly into light grey, Stay Press trousers. He appears upright and casual with his top button undone. He has a shiny bald head with angular cheek bones and a sharply chiselled chin. A pair of thin metal glasses wrap round his brow, framing his emotionless grey eyes in cold perfection.

He takes a seat at his desk. The window behind him overlooks Hammersmith: a mess of red-fired clay and dirty slate roofs fill the vista.

"Please take a seat," the doctor says, showing them to two plastic chairs next to his desk. He turns his head to engage with a computer screen displaying an image of a captured circle.

"So, as we can see here," the doctor says, pointing a yellow Bic pen at the screen, "this is the lining of the prostate gland."

"Are you German?" Simon interrupts the doctor, who stops and raises his eyebrows carefully.

"Yes, I was brought up in Duisburg before my family moved back out into the country," says the doctor.

Simon is confused by the expression on Dr Untermeyer's face. "My grandfather went to Duisburg once," he says.

"I see," the doctor replies, turning his eyes back to the screen.

Sonia squeezes Simon's hand.

"So, Mr Radcliffe, if you look around the wall of the prostate here," Dr Untermeyer traces his pen around the MRI scan and stops at an irregular fuzzy shape clinging to the lining of the gland.

"This —" the doctor tries to continue, but Simon interrupts him again.

"He didn't come back from Duisburg."

"If you wish to talk about your grandfather, Simon, I am the wrong kind of doctor."

"It's cancer isn't it?" Simon says.

"Yes, you have been unlucky."

"We are trying to have a baby," imparts Sonia dolefully.

"I see," the doctor answers, with no show of emotion.

The three sit in silence while the circular MRI scan stares into the room like an eyeless amoeba. A thick ball of watery salt accelerates down Sonia's cheek before splattering into little droplets on the edge of her plastic chair.

"It is possible to freeze sperm before you have the operation," the doctor informs them frankly.

"Operation?" Simon replies sharply.

"Yes, you are lucky," the doctor says.

"A few seconds ago you said I was unlucky," Simon replies, exasperated.

"It's true. You have been unlucky. But you are also very lucky." Dr Untermeyer stumbles through his sentence, tripping on the tracks delivering his train of thought.

"We can still have a baby then?" Sonia croaks.

"You have a chance at life," says the doctor.

The German accent is starting to annoy Simon. "Do you mean me, or the baby?" he says.

"A Macmillan nurse will help with any further questions. I will be passing your case on to the head surgeon. He is very good. The best in the world, they say."

"Thank you for your help today," musters Sonia.

A Macmillan nurse, trained in caring for cancer patients, meets them at the door of Dr Untermeyer's office and leads them quickly to another room. Simon remembers nothing she says, only that she had white hair and scaly skin. He's fortunate that Sonia listens carefully and even takes some leaflets away.

11

Back To The Grill Again

Another cold, wet Wednesday morning and the semi-circle of men have reformed in the shape of a slice of lemon before a slightly bedraggled-looking Liz. Tobias is here wearing his grey leather sandals. Simon glances outside, feeling uncomfortable that the man who seems to be in his business is back again. The path outside glistens, reflecting the clouds' white light. It's definitely still cold and wet.

Liz goes over the list on the blackboard again. Fresh chalk squeaks as she underlines acceptance with a capital A. The chalk snaps and rolls onto the floor. She goes to bend over. Then she doesn't.

"OK, can we all stand up and close our eyes," she says.

Everybody does.

"I want you all to loosen up, shake your shoulders, move your legs up and down." She leads them with her own physical actions. Andy looks like a greasy mopped scarecrow incapacitated in a chill out tent. Tony dances robotically to a high speed rhythm in his head. Rupert barely moves but at least he's trying. Wilf just stands still. Simon decides on a few squat thrusts and Robert does some wobbly Elvis leg.

Robert passes wind in something close to a perfect C.

The room becomes a pressure cooker of suppressed laughter.

"It's OK. This is to be expected. It's natural when we open up together," Liz says, catching her professional self from falling.

The smell is ferocious: a few of the group gag.

Liz heads over to open the windows and vehicle fumes come rushing in. "So, does anybody know the meaning of the word acceptance?" she says, moving them on with an easy starter for ten. "Acceptance can mean that we are prepared to adapt to the needs and differences of others but also adapt to the needs within ourselves. Can anyone think of things they have had to accept?"

Tony stirs. "The thing is, I haven't told you, but I had to come out. You know, tell folk I was gay. It was in my twenties and that was both types — accepting people were going to hate me, then accepting it was me, who I was myself, who I'd always been." Tony has his tattooed right hand planted firmly on his heart.

Chairs squeak like mice trapped in the bin.

"I was rejected by my father for not being a 'real man'. The only people who got me were the lads I met through the fighting," Tony continues, and the mood shifts again. "Yeah, I know. It's not what you would expect. I was running with the boys in the ICF."

"The paint manufacturers?" Robert quips.

Feeling lost, Liz stares at Tony, but the rest of the group know. The West Ham United top that Tony wore at the last session was a dead giveaway.

"So," says Simon, with a bemused tone in his voice, "you travelled on trains to various towns in England with hooligans of the Inter City Firm, trying to hurt people in pre-organized violence, and you're gay?"

"You sound like a copper," observes Robert.

"Wouldn't they all want to kick your lips off?" adds Andy with his eyebrows crushed into a bewildered look.

"Have you seen the size of him?" Wilf notes, grabbing his own arms for comfort.

"It wasn't only trains," says Tony. "Some of the time it was coaches. The ICF were the first people to accept me for who I was. The only trouble came from the other crews and the rucking."

"Who was the hardest then?" Wilf asks Tony, and Liz cuts him off.

"Thanks, Tony. It was very brave of you to share that experience with us." She nods at him and pauses with her eyes closed.

"Rupert, do you have any stories of acceptance you can share with us?" Liz asks.

Rupert raises his gaze from the floor for the first time and barks like a dog. A single laugh from Robert gets snorted back into a cough and Rupert begins.

"IIIIIt's like when you find a group of old school friends online and you send a request to join the group and the people administering the page ddon't accept your request."

Because Rupert rarely speaks, Simon finds his quiet, stuttering voice has the effect of encouraging the emotional content to sink in deeply, like warm sun cream.

"So, you go into the list of mmmembers and pick out some people you remember as nice people," Rupert continues. "One guy in the group had stopped me being bullied at school. And you send a friend request but it never gggggggets accepted."

Rupert's eyes appear increasingly glassy, darting from side

to side as he struggles with more than one issue at the same time. "And, I've never had a girlfriend."

"OK," whispers Liz in a voice that feels like the audio version of a hug.

"Then you have to accept that people don't like you, that they're too cruel to separate the difference between a medical condition and what's in here," says Rupert, his words flowing as both of his index fingers point to the centre of his chest.

"Maybe your old friends had just moved on, Rupert?" Liz offers in support.

"There's no space to move on in a digital world. We're all trapped inside our phones," Rupert replies, staring back at the floor.

"The problem with reality is that it's all too much for anyone to process," adds Simon, trying to mix philosophy with empathy.

"Perhaps altruism is selfishness in disguise?" Tobias weighs in, the two purple amethysts on his gold pin badge glowing like purple eyes.

"Helping others is the basis of all societies," Liz responds.

"Not true of Sparta, of course," says Tobias. "But sometimes we can transcend simple acts of help and become a force for good, and in turn a deeper healing can be found. The past can be repaired through positive action and acts of love."

Simon thinks he sounds like a pastor.

"Fucking hippy!" shouts Robert with a snide laugh.

"We all like to think in clichés but perhaps cliché is the most dangerous thought of all, Robert," Tobias continues. "It's hard to change shape when we are told there is nothing more than the cages we put ourselves in."

"You're talking rubbish. Who are you anyway?" says Robert.

"That's enough, Robert. Tobias is our guest," interjects Liz.

"Guest?" Simon raises his eyebrows and wonders if Tobias has bothered anyone else in the group on their way home from Rings and Things.

Andy sits up in his seat to join in. "I thought you could only come here if you were sent by a doctor."

"Maybe he's the doctor," offers Wilf.

"Now then, gentlemen," says Liz. "Time is moving on. I wanted to talk today about tinnitus as I know it bothers you all to different degrees." She moves to the other side of the blackboard.

Wilf gives Liz a desperate look. "Is it possible to have surgery to remove the continuous sound inside of your ears?"

"There is nothing that the medical world can do to eradicate tinnitus at the moment," Liz replies. "Some people find it comes and goes. Some learn to live with it through adaptation."

"What about the ones who top themselves?" asks Robert with a sneer.

"They've learned to not live with it," Wilf says.

Simon has stopped listening again. There's a definite time limit to concentrating on other people's problems, unless you are a parent, he thinks, and even they must get a lot of it wrong. Perhaps that's the issue: just other people, full stop. Arranging music in his head moves Simon's own troubles to the side, pushes them back down into the depths of his mind.

In a detached daze he finds himself on autopilot and on the bus home again. Tomorrow he will be having his sperm frozen.

"Just in case," Sonia keeps telling him.

"Just in case," he keeps replying with decreasing conviction.

He plays the scene of her saying it to him over and over in his head.

"Just in case."

12

Frozen Tadpoles

It's 10 a.m. and Simon arrives early at the carved stone entrance of the Shepherd's Bush Medical Centre. He passes through the permanently revolving doors and into a narrow corridor lined with blue linoleum. Walking by the unhealthy snack dispensary found in the entrance of every hospital, he finds a charity shop lurking down an alley within one of the wards.

Digging for vinyl might help kill time before his 10:30 appointment in the andrology department. The charity shop is set out like a poverty-stricken pop star's walk-in wardrobe. A rack of old coats and shirts are pushed into a corner on broken wheels. In the middle of the shop a volunteer with silver blue hair mans the till, surrounded by a row of perished rubber Wellingtons. Jigsaw puzzles, teapots, nylon sportswear and dead men's shoes litter the floor. There is no vinyl. A solitary Steps CD is leaning against the bottom of an aluminium frame walker.

Simon leaves the charity shop and takes a right turn down the corridor and follows the signs for andrology. After a hundred yards, a white door with frosted glass appears on his right. He grips the handle, twists and enters the cramped room filled with yesterday's air. He reports at a small kiosk where a dozy-eyed balding man in a nylon burgundy shirt takes his name. He sinks into one of the faux leather sofas and picks idly at the brown material sticking up from the arm like loose fake skin. The waiting room has three doors lined up on one side.

A boy with a cream complexion, probably in his twenties, sits alongside his partner tapping his index finger against his thumb. Maybe the young man is going to die of something awful soon. He doesn't look ill, though.

Simon catches his own reflection in the idle TV bolted to the wall; he doesn't look ill, either. Lots of people don't look ill before they die, especially gun shot or car crash victims.

"Mr. Radcliffe," the secretary chirps in a Kiwi accent, the deep lines in his face moving in unison.

"Yes," Simon replies, slightly startled. He gives his head a shake.

"Can you come in, please?" he says, holding the door with his lumpy knuckled hand and stepping to the side. "I'm Mr Bellway, the andrology department secretary." He offers Simon a red plastic chair next to a cramped desk and goes through his paperwork.

The lack of fresh air has triggered a sense of doom. "Is he going to die as well?" Simon asks quietly so only Mr Bellway can hear.

"Die?" says Mr Bellway, his Kiwi accent distorting the word.

"The lad in there. He's so young," says Simon, fidgeting with his trouser pockets. He notices a sticker stuck on the iron filing cabinet behind Mr Bellway. On the sticker is a red-eyed creature cut from stone on a crest that reads: Ake Ake Kia Kaha. "I mean, it's just not fair. My wife has about two years left to find another man if I pop the old clogs."

"Sorry, Mr Radcliffe. I'm not sure what you mean. And, anyway, we can't discuss other people's information," Mr Bellway replies tersely.

"I'll shut up then."

"So, do you have a date?" Mr Bellway asks, eyes peering over his black-rimmed NHS reading glasses.

Simon leans forward. "A date for what?"

"A date for the operation," Mr Bellway says.

"I'm not sure if I'm having an operation. I've not heard anything back yet." Simon wishes the thought forward wistfully, fighting against the rush of reality closing in.

Mr Bellway peers at him almost triumphantly. "It seems that you have one scheduled, according to the papers sent over by the urology department."

"It's always nice to know these things in advance, so you can show up on time," Simon replies with raised eyebrows, his guts tingling.

"Yes, let's get this sample done now then."

"Are we in that much of a hurry?" Simon's pulse is racing faster than his thoughts.

"I don't know," says Mr Bellway. "I don't have all of your paperwork. Can you tell me, what's your problem again?"

"Prostate."

"Ah, yes. Quite common."

Simon lets out a sigh as Mr Bellway hands him a jar.

"Will you need material?" adds Mr Bellway.

"Pardon?" says Simon.

"Stimulus," Mr Bellway says, in evident distaste.

"No, thank you. I've made a career out of my imagination," Simon replies, holding the jar tightly with both hands in his lap.

The secretary points to show him the way. "It's the first one on your right."

Simon heads in and shuts the door behind him. In front of him is a plastic covered bed. He looks down at the container in his hand, checks the time on his watch, and wonders how much time he's got left for everything.

13

Before the Ice Age

Friday night. Sonia and Simon are sat in the lounge drinking tea. Sonia turns the television off and they both put down their phones.

"The doctor at Guys said they'll move our second round of IVF, so it doesn't clash with your operation," says Sonia. "We've got to stay positive." The overhead light catching her golden-brown skin reminds Simon of that night he met her at the party in Willesden, before things got so complicated.

"Can your body take all those injections again? It's so soon after the last time," says Simon, his forehead crumpled up with concern.

"They said it's OK to go again on my next cycle. We'll have more chance if they don't use sperm that's been frozen," says Sonia gently.

"What else do I have to do?" says Simon, feeling lost in the pile up of information.

"Live. And eat as healthily as possible. You've done it before. You just have to learn how to keep it that way."

"That last andrology place in Shepherds Bush, it was terrible, reeked of desperation — death even." Simon shivers with the memory.

"It's good that it got sorted out now, honey. You might not be the same after the operation. Joanna's husband John went on a strict avocado and almond diet. He did suffer from a very low libido though. At least that's never been a problem for you," says Sonia.

"I wouldn't know about that. Have you read the side effects list on the letter?" Simon asks while shuffling the very same paperwork in his hands nervously.

"Yes, I know, sweetheart." Sonia sighs.

"I might not... I might not get an erection again." Simon stares down at the letter with a blank look on his pale face.

Sonia moves over to hug Simon in his chair. "You know I love you whatever happens."

"I suppose I've had a good run." He inhales fast to push back the feeling rising in his chest.

"Through thick and thin," Sonia says, echoing their day in church.

"The hard and the slim," Simon says, laughing through his pressured exhale.

"I know, darling. It's not funny," Sonia says, crushing the letter between them.

Simon sighs deeply. "What else could it be, though? I'm getting sick of thinking."

"Don't think, just be." She kisses the salty water on his cheeks. "You're going to be alright. I know it because I can feel that we're going to be OK. It's as if somebody is watching out for us." Sonia starts running her fingers through his hair.

"I don't want our kid to be a Catholic. Too much apologizing. It's bad enough being English as it is," says Simon.

"I don't mean God is watching out for us," Sonia whispers. "I mean some other kind of force wants us to have a baby."

Simon shakes his head at the thought and brings it all back down to brass tacks. "Exactly how long will we have?"

"Three weeks. I've already started injecting. A new batch of hormones arrived yesterday."

Sonia points over to the fridge as Simon's phone rings. It's his mum, Anne. Her dulcet Geordie tone radiates a sense of peace, giving Simon spirit, strength and hope. He misses home.

"I've been thinking of you both," says Anne. "How are you getting on?"

"Everything is great, Mum. We got another chance to go and try for a baby again."

"How is Sonia bearing up?"

"Good, Mum. I've been making you a playlist. Every time I hear Billy Joel it reminds me that I really need to get it done."

Sonia shouts, "Hi, Anne! We miss you!" as she opens the fridge door, shaking the bottles of hormones clinking against each other.

"I'm trying to find a picture of my father," Anne tells Simon. "We've never had one, as you know, since Grandma Jean lost his service picture. She went a little mad for a while, I suppose. Grief can do that to anyone."

"I'm sorry, Mum," says Simon. "I can't imagine not knowing what your dad looks like."

"Thank you, son. In any case, the Royal Grammar School is going to hold a service for former pupils lost in the two wars. Picture or no picture, it would be wonderful if you could come. But I know you've both got a lot on."

14

Second Time Around

A new batch of eggs are now in prime shape, ready for harvest in the hospital. This is Simon and Sonia's final free round of IVF. The treatment has been moved forward a month to account for Simon's prostate operation. The baby making will take place in a petri dish at Guy's Hospital by the dirty brown banks of the old river Thames.

Simon has managed to increase his sperm count after the doctor likened his first sample to irradiated porridge; now they're approaching the business end of in vitro sex. Simon and Sonia are sat in the hospital's fertility waiting room. A couple sat next to them are pressing their palms together, praying in unison for the unimaginable glory of a wailing infant.

At the end of the corridor, behind locked doors, awaits a hushed room — the place where everything happens on the inside. A bubbly red-haired nurse in a white uniform and matching hair net appears in the window. She presses a big green button and the doors become temporarily penetrable. Simon and Sonia are ushered in and taken to a corner of the ward where they go behind a big blue curtain and find a bed on wheels, with crisp white sheets, waiting for them.

"Can you confirm your name, please?" says the nurse, who

appeared from a door, marked Lab, at the end of the room.

"Sonia Radcliffe."

"And is this your husband?" the nurse asks, eyes down as she scribbles away with their paperwork on a worn clipboard.

"Yes, that's me," Simon answers with a nervous smile, in a voice reminiscent of a lost game show host.

Soon Sonia will be injected with knock-out juice and wheeled into a room that Simon won't be allowed to see. Inside the airtight theatre a stranger will harvest Sonia's eggs and prepare each one for injection with a single sperm. A microscope will be used to locate the healthiest looking member of Simon's genetic future. What could be the very last of his chosen few will be sucked up into a miniature glass needle and javelined in.

Inside the ward, another couple hide behind the curtains that wrap around their beds, whispering with an underlying hint of tension. The hum of the air conditioning blends effortlessly with the constant ringing haunting Simon's ears, scratching away at his thoughts, reminding him of all the losses when he thought he would win. His low-slung remix of Dean Martin's "Baby, It's Cold Outside" springs to mind. The remix had earned Capitol Records millions, but he'd been stiffed on the contract and took a tiny one-off fee. So it goes.

The nurse asks Sonia to undress and put a gown on.

"Excuse me, sir," says another nurse who has appeared in a green uniform with a hair net. "We need you to provide the sample now."

Simon swallows drily. "Where do you want me?"

"In the room over there, by the sink, sir," the nurse in the green hair net points at a white door and hands him a plastic container with a screw top.

"Just leave it in the box on the left and press the buzzer when you're done." The nurse heads back through some hermetically sealed doors at the end of the room.

Inside the prison cell sample room, Simon feels wholly unprepared. A metallic desk in the corner has a surface finished with a plastic cream veneer. He unzips and whispers "please". It's going to cost them twenty grand if he can't conjure an accurate orgasm. After next week's prostate operation, he might have to hire another man in.

"God help me," he prays. "Save the last wank for me."

Underneath the desk a rusty looking drawer has a smudged sticker across its front. He opens it to the sound of screeching metal and looks anxiously over his shoulder. Inside the drawer, a stash of antique pornographic magazines lies crumpled with thumbed corners. Simon can't bear to touch the covers. He uses two pens like chopsticks to pluck the magazines from the draw and they drop with a slap onto the floor. He hates the noise. Outside, beyond the door, everyone knows exactly what he's doing — struggling to throttle an untamed goose he's been strangling for the best part of a lifetime, again.

Simon flicks the pages over with a pen, hoping for a glimmer of inspiration. These havens are highly unshaven and most of the girls on display will be grandmothers; shuffled off their knickers and mortal coils.

Despite the outdated images, nature has gifted Simon the ability to masturbate under pressure. In his head, the Queen bass line kicks in. Just as the chords join the production, a twisted mix of fantasy and memory merge in Simon's mind and, with a hopeless shudder, he dispatches the biological prize into the medical receptacle.

Simon drags the magazines back into the draw and drops

the viscous data into the collection box with a sense of relieved dishevelment. He presses the exit buzzer with his elbow and suppresses the urge to shout, "Oi, wanker! You're up next."

Simon re-enters the ward sheepishly and focuses his eyes on the laboratory doors that lead to Sonia. Behind him, he hears another buzzer. A nurse has come out of an office and taken Simon's sample from the collection box. He sees her hand it through the door to another person, presumably a doctor, who is out of sight. Just before the nurse closes the door behind her, Simon sees a lab coat draped across a chair. The coat's lapel has a golden pin with two ruby eyes shining in the strip lights. The eyes on the pin flash as a bony hand picks up the lab coat.

15

Can You Feel It?
That Burning Sensation

It's 9:40 on a Tuesday morning. The egg that was "put back" into Sonia ten days ago has implanted into her womb. Now, it's Simon's turn for a procedure. He arrives with trepidation at Charing Cross Hospital for his prostate cancer operation. This time they will be knocking him out properly. Simon is led to the same pre-op room on the third floor. He gets undressed and puts on a cape. A tall male nurse with hairy hands, light brown eyes and a face mask wheels him into a holding bay. A nurse lowers the back of the bed down.

A slim female anaesthetist, who introduces herself as Dr Frau Brandt, appears to Simon's right. She asks him a few simple questions in a soft German accent, inserting a giant cannula into the top of his hand as she speaks. Simon grits his teeth and apologizes for something he's not quite sure of, as he loses consciousness in the blink of an eye. His last memory is of the doctor smiling at him, her hand holding his, softly stroking his fingers with a strange sense of affection.

Simon wakes as though someone has plugged him back into the mains. He's staring at white squares of polystyrene on the ceiling. As his senses return, he looks down under the thin sheet and sees he has a two-centimetre thick catheter hanging out of his waterworks. He moves his leg to the side and a yellow nozzle with a green tap falls out of the side of his cape. A nurse helps Simon to get dressed, strapping the catheter to the side of his left leg with a strip of white elastic.

He exits the ward, navigating the rotating doors, and limps down Fulham Palace Road to Hammersmith station. He catches a train home and exits at Brondesbury Park. On the platform he thumps the lift's disabled button for a ride up to street level. He walks down the avenue toward his flat with a bow-legged gait.

Once inside, he drops the white paper bag bulging with post-op antibiotics on the kitchen counter, collapses fully clothed on the lounge sofa, and sleeps for the rest of the afternoon. He wakes to the sound of Sonia's key in the door.

Sonia sits down next to him and picks up his hand, leading him to the bathroom in silence. It all seems like a dream until he feels the dig of the catheter tap scraping against his knee.

"Are you feeling alright?" she says. "How was today?"

"It's pretty much a blank, although I did have a dream of floating in the air and landing on a roof. I didn't think that was possible under anaesthetic." Simon looks out of it.

"I've been beside myself worrying about you. My boss wouldn't let me come back any earlier," Sonia says while positioning herself on the toilet. "I'm so sorry — I wish I could have been there for you for the whole day."

"What are you doing?" Simon asks.

"It's time to do the test, honey. Come, let's read it together."

"I have to go," says Simon, in a panic.

Sonia finishes peeing on the pen and leaps up to get out

of the way so Simon can use the loo. Simon fumbles with the catheter tap, turns it and a stream of raspberry pink flows out. He feels her catching him and she holds him upright against the bathroom radiator.

"Honey, we're pregnant!" she tells him beaming.

Simon bends forward to be sick in the sink.

16

Attendance Mission

Simon has to suppress the urge not to return to group counselling: everything is looking up. Sonia is pregnant — although she does keep reminding him not to tell anyone until they get past the three-month mark. For now, it seems he's dodged nature's attempt at premature death. Even though his ears keep ringing, life feels a whole lot better. But, having missed the last two weeks of Rings and Things, he's found himself missing his new acquaintances. Perhaps he should be calling them friends. Sharing their thoughts had made him feel a little happier; they were like a gang, bonding over failure.

Simon used to have black periods when he missed more than just people; he missed absolutely everything, even the places he'd never been to and the things he'd never seen. He got very good at making pointless thoughts join together, invisible thinking swarmed his mind like blue bottles dancing round unpalatable pieces of his past. Then there were the manic times that looked fantastic from the outside but burned great holes into the fabric of his soul.

At first the doctor suggested he use a Jal Neti pot to wash out his sinus cavities, but the problem was beyond his face, behind the bones. It was in his chemistry. An imbalance in the mix of his blancmange, as his doctor had so strangely put it.

Rings and Things has started the process of repairing him; it has given Simon something that he wasn't aware that he had lost.

"Liz, do you mind if we put 'connection' on the board," Simon asks politely.

"Of course, Simon. It encompasses a few words we already have up here, I suppose. Good choice," Liz replies.

Simon looks around the empty portacabin. "It's a shame I'm the only one who turned up today."

"Yes, it is, especially considering we have a guest talk from the National Happy Service mental health team."

The door of the portacabin opens and Dr Frau Brandt walks in. The ice-cold feeling Simon felt during the biopsy appears again, spreading from the depths of his body and moving out to the tips of his fingers like a frost setting in. His grandfather Jack had flown at night and his grandmother Jean had told Simon that, no matter how much clothing she had sent, Jack could never keep warm at 20,000 feet.

His phone rings as Dr Frau Brandt shakes Liz's hand by the blackboard. He picks up the phone. It's his father, Peter.

"Hello, son!" Peter bellows in a snappy tone. Simon puts his hand over the receiver.

"I'm sorry. I'll have to take this." Simon heads out of the portacabin and puts his hand over his ear to hide the noise of the busy roundabout.

"Hi, Dad. How are you both?"

"Good, son. I wanted to tell you there's a ceremony at the Royal Grammar School in Jesmond next week. They're going to add a family member's name to the school alumni roll call."

"Mum mentioned it."

"Yes, it's really something that should have been done a long time ago. We're still not having any luck tracking down a picture of your grandad Jack, mind you. It would mean so much to your mum if we could find some kind of memento before the ceremony."

"I'll keep looking out for one online, Dad. But I just can't come home at the moment. There's too much going on."

After some pleasantries and a hurried goodbye, Simon concludes the call and looks through the window of the portacabin. Liz and Dr Frau Brandt are deep in conversation. He wonders if they're talking about his prostate, and whether any of the other guys in the group had surgery, with Dr Frau in attendance. He's starting to feel as if everyone is performing a double service, leading double lives. Watching them for a minute or two longer, he tries to decipher their words, then turns on his heels and heads for home without saying goodbye.

17

Scanning the Horizon

Simon and Sonia haven't stopped hugging. They've freshened the high Edwardian ceilings and walls of the spare room with a five-litre tub of white paint.

It's been six weeks since Sonia took the pregnancy test on the evening of Simon's operation. Today they will visit Guy's and St Thomas for their first scan. Sonia says they'll be able to see a heartbeat, have a chance to see their baby — at least that's what the nurse told her over the phone. On the journey to the hospital, Simon gets excited thinking about how their baby will learn all about music. He and Sonia can barely hear each other over the screech of the steel wheels of the Jubilee line. But he can't stop garbling about how the songs he plays will affect their baby's heart rate.

The T-shaped waiting area is empty. BBC News is playing quietly on a TV just out of sight. The door of the examination room opens with a burst of life and a beaming couple in their mid-thirties appear. The woman has a printout of her scan in her hand; she lifts the black and white ticket of joy to her lips and kisses a picture of their newly written future. Simon and Sonia smile at the couple bouncing triumphantly down the brightly lit corridor.

A sonographer appears in a dark blue trouser suit, introduces herself as Nurse Mulligan, and welcomes them into the air-conditioned examination room with her thick outstretched arm. A bed surrounded by ultrasound equipment dominates the room's centre and three consultancy chairs are set up as two facing one. Nurse Mulligan asks Sonia to sit on the fresh white paper rolled out across the bed. Sonia complies and lifts up her top, revealing her skin. Nurse Mulligan smears Sonia's stomach with a clear gel and Sonia gasps.

"It's so cold!" Sonia says, smiling nervously.

Nurse Mulligan apologizes and places a high frequency probe against Sonia's glistening torso. The screen at the side of the bed shows a circle like the clouded surface of Jupiter. The nurse presses down and distorted shapes come in and out of focus, like squashed aliens, as she pushes and pulls the probe back and forth.

"How is our baby looking?" asks Sonia.

"I'm just trying to find the embryonic sac," replies Nurse Mulligan.

"We watched some footage of ultrasounds online together, last night," says Sonia.

"Yes, yes we did," says Simon, eyes focused on the screen intently.

"I'm getting a sign here of the sac." Nurse Mulligan points at the bubble amongst the clouds of planet womb, the sac's tiny shape changing with the movements of the probe. The bubble is just a bubble. "But I'm really sorry. I'm afraid I'm having trouble detecting a heartbeat. It might mean a number of things..."

A swell starts up in Simon's stomach.

"So, there isn't a baby?" Sonia says with a crack in her voice.

"I can only find the embryonic sac."

"What happened to our baby?" Simon asks in disbelief.

"Please, wipe your tummy off and I will explain." The nurse hands Sonia some rough paper towel and she wipes the ultrasound gel from her stomach.

Simon and Sonia sit side-by-side in the two red plastic chairs.

Nurse Mulligan sits in the single grey chair and sighs.

"Twenty per cent of pregnancies end this way. It's called a blighted ovum," she says.

"It was a fake baby then," Simon says, his words spluttering out.

"If it's any consolation, in your case the body has likely made this decision correctly," the nurse says, trying to comfort them.

"But that was our last free go," says Simon ruefully, remembering from now on the process comes at a financial cost on top of everything else. Immediately, however, he knew his timing was off. That was the last thing Sonia would be wanting to think about that that moment.

"I'm sorry. Sorry for your loss," says Nurse Mulligan.

The couple stand up, gripping each other's hands. As they leave the office, Simon hears the nurse pick up the phone: "Dr Untermeyer's office, please."

18

Runout Groove

"Money, money, money," the ABBA lyrics fill the library room of the Ilithios Members Club. Simon is back at work playing music he doesn't like to people he has no connection with. He's sat awkwardly on a bar stool behind the record decks, hiding his catheter with a record sleeve.

The library room is packed. Two grey-haired women wearing black leather pants, green velvet jackets and tiaras gyrate against each other for the pleasure of four tall Belgian businessmen who aren't paying any attention. The bar staff weave their way skilfully among the crowd, holding their trays of drinks above the members' expensive outfits, and sweating through their uniforms.

The music will have to be extraordinarily bad tonight — the busier it gets, the more the barrel gets scraped. At the end of the night Simon asks Patryk to help him down the stairs with his records. Simon's surgeon told him not to carry anything heavier than a melon for six weeks, without telling him exactly which kind. His vinyl weighs substantially more than a pair of oversized watermelons.

Outside, the beggars wait for the staggering stragglers to catch cabs. A ruddy-faced homeless man with ulcers and straw-coloured matted hair shows Simon a card trick.

Simon tries to avoid the emotional fly trap closing around him. "I don't have any money to give you, I'm sorry," he says.

"But you watched the trick," the homeless man says in a croaky voice, his gin-dipped lips glistening in the streetlights overhead.

"I know. I'm sorry. But it seemed rude to look away," Simon replies unconvincingly.

"People find it easy to be rude when you sit on the pavement. The world is filled with the temporarily blind, yet it's the artist's job to never look away," the homeless man croaks.

"I'm sorry," says Simon again, feeling tired and overwhelmed by the observation.

The homeless man points his blackened finger toward the Santander Bank next to the Rough Trade record shop. "There's a cash machine over the road," he says.

"I know, but I can't carry the boxes over there. I'm a bit hamstrung at the moment." Simon taps at his catheter-strapped leg.

"I'll look after them for you. Go on. It'll only take a minute," the homeless man says, encouraging Simon with a flick of his wrist.

Simon gives in to his conscience and crosses the road. The blue neon light of the London Dry brewery reflects up from a puddle as he limps toward the metal cash dispenser set back into the wall. He pulls his wallet out, removes his bank card and types in his pin. Crossing the road with a crisp five-pound note curled up in his hand, he looks at the empty street at the entrance of the Ilithios. The homeless man and his record boxes have gone. All that is left is an empty bottle of London Dry Gin.

19

The Digital Fruit Store

Simon will struggle to make money without gigs. His work at the Ilithios club is occasionally regular. The box of curated dancefloor vinyl stolen on Portobello Road would cost him thousands to replace. It's time for him to go digital.

He takes the Overground train to the Westfield shopping centre in Shepherds Bush. Entering the glass stadium of corporate dreams, he jumps on an elevator heading up to the first floor where the Apple sign is glowing warm against the brushed steel shop front that beckons him in. Simon approaches the back of the shop and engages with a member of the staff, a kid assistant with delicate flawless skin sitting innocently atop his freckle gilded cheekbones. They talk about home recording techniques for a while, then Simon dives in.

"So, if I record all the vinyl into the computer, will I have those songs in there, with easy access at a high bit rate?" Simon asks the assistant as he points a finger at a fifteen-inch MacBook Pro, tied with metal cable to the table in front of them.

"Yes, sir, they'd be saved as WAV files if you so wished," replies the assistant, his chestnut eyes gleaming under the display lights. "And many more songs are available through a wide range of digital distribution services."

"Can you get rarities and things that no one else has?" Simon prods the assistant with the blunted tip of his wilting DJ ego.

"I'm not sure, sir. If you don't mind me asking, why would you want that?" the assistant says.

"To be good you have to be different," says Simon with a sense of pride poking distastefully above the parapet.

"I see, sir. But if nobody knows the songs, are they going to care?" the assistant asks with a look of concern.

"Have you ever been to a club?" Simon squints like a pound shop Clint Eastwood.

"Yes, a while back," the assistant answers brightly.

"How old are you?" Simon steps back a few feet.

"Twenty-two," the assistant replies.

"Well it's not just about the dancing," Simon sighs as the decades press against his diaphragm.

"What else is it about, sir?"

"Making time disappear," Simon answers triumphantly.

"I'm not with you, sorry." The assistant turns his head to signal for help from the members of staff hovering round the Genius Bar like fruit flies.

"OK, that's your loss then," Simon blurts out.

"We do have lossless files as well, sir," the assistant says.

Simon assumes the kid has suddenly remembered his sales bonus. "A homeless man stole all my DJ vinyl," he explains pathetically.

"I'm sorry. That's bad. He must have been a fast mover."

"I was incapacitated by empathy and I can't lift anything heavier than a watermelon. Anyway, this software, will it allow me to mix the records together like vinyl?" Simon cuts to the chase.

"The software will mix the records together for you. It has a feature called sync," the assistant says, explaining the function that allows preschool children and farm animals to beat match perfectly.

"Sorry?" Simon replies, the colour draining from his face.

"Are you OK, sir?" asks the assistant, reaching to touch his elbow with the palm of his hand. "You've gone a funny colour. What did you have for lunch?"

"My self-respect," Simon replies, his eyes burning through the MacBook before him.

The assistant shrugs as the colour slowly returns to Simon's cheeks. "I don't understand," he says. "Do you want the equipment or not?"

"All of our lives, our meanings and values have been stolen by an algorithm," Simon says, offering his words to the Apple store like he was on stage at the Old Vic.

"But it's just other people's music," says the assistant.

"Ah, forget it. I'll have it then," says Simon, knowing it will cost him all the money he's earned from his last few months of Ilithios gigs — money he'd told Sonia he would save for emergencies, while she'd been picking up all their bills.

He limps out of the store gripping the translucent bag filled with digital dreams.

At the bus stop, his phone rings just as a bus arrives. It's his father, Peter. Simon fumbles with his Oyster card, clamping the phone between his shoulder and chin while Peter explains he'd like help with setting up an eBay account. Simon smiles, thinking of his mother's joy if his dad's wild collection of historical items were to be sent off to new homes. But, no, apparently there's a rare set of plotting compasses from a Lancaster bomber and Peter just has to have them.

20

The Gift

It's Wednesday in Wembley, time for another Rings & Things. It's a chance for Simon to apologize to Liz for disappearing last time. Sonia hasn't been allowed anytime off work despite the miscarriage; it's driving Simon crazy. He has tried to keep her mentally occupied with offers of a trip to the cinema, but she doesn't want to come out to play. Sonia told Simon she nearly let it slip to human resources that they were trying for a baby. To keep her mind off it, she had ordered Simon two pairs of loose jogging pants from Jacamo in the paltry thirty minutes allowed for her lunch. He's chosen to wear the yellow ones today.

Exiting the bus with a stumble, he burps away his travel sickness and enters the portacabin just as the session is about to begin.

"Hammer time!" shouts Robert as Simon limps over to an empty chair in the semi-circle.

"Sorry I'm a bit late, everyone," Simon addresses the room, his face turning a little pink. "Please begin."

"Have you been drinking?" asks Robert.

"No, Robert. It's a long story," Simon whispers.

"We missed you the last few weeks, Simon," Liz says with a broad smile, her hands clasped firmly together.

"I missed you all, too, and I'm sorry for last time, Liz." Simon smiles and acknowledges them one by one with a nod.

Liz puts her index finger on her lips and Simon wonders if it was a secret Dr Frau had come that time, with nobody in attendance but him.

"Is everything alright?" Andy asks, staring at Simon's legs.

"Minor operation. Nothing to worry about. I just have to wear silly pants for a while." Simon sits himself down with a groan. "Anyway, where were all of you the other week?"

"It was cancelled because Liz was sick, and they couldn't get a replacement in," Wilf informs him.

"I see, I see." Simon stares at Liz, who shakes her head quickly.

"Alright, gentleman. Let's get a start," says Liz, and they move on. Simon is obsessing over the words on the board, starting to feel they were written as hidden messages, just for him.

The session drifts along. Simon just can't concentrate; he's decided to confront Liz about the anaesthetist, Frau Brandt, turning up at the ghost session created for him. He waits for Liz at the end of the session and sidles up to her chair next to the blackboard. Suddenly, they are alone.

"I'm sorry I couldn't stay last time, Liz," Simon tells her with his head bowed.

"That's alright, Simon. These things happen."

"Why were you meeting with the woman who knocked me out in Charing Cross Hospital?"

"Sorry, Simon?"

"That woman you were with, she injected me, put me under, stroked my hand."

"I don't choose who the Happy Service send over, Simon. She came with a very good recommendation as a Tinnitus Therapy specialist."

"As well as being an anaesthetist?"

"Again, I don't choose who they send over or the timetable, Simon."

"Why did you tell the rest of the group you were ill, then?"

Liz smiles at him and taps her finger on the cardboard cover of her lesson plan. "It was probably a mistake, Simon. The team who manage my rota get things wrong now and again."

"Liz, look at these words on the board. Did you put them here for me?" Simon points at The Past, moves his finger over Anger and rests it on Belonging.

"Don't be silly, Simon. These words are for everybody. This is all group therapy — that's the whole point of Rings and Things. Now if you don't mind, I have to meet a friend in an hour and the Jubilee line is running slow."

Liz lifts herself out of her plastic chair and they walk together across the floor sticky with spilled coffee. They stand on the metal steps of the portacabin. Liz locks the door and Simon offers an unconvincing goodbye. He takes the bus home. Tobias is sat next to him again. Simon puts his head in his hands and stares at the floor.

"Have you heard of the saying, 'dirty hands clean money'?" Tobias asks as the bus weaves through Willesden.

"No," Simon replies, pulling at his yellow pants, which are trapped between the cheeks of his bruised backside.

"Do you like to gamble?"

"No, I don't," Simon replies flatly.

"So why do you dedicate so much time pretending that

you're a musician, stealing other people's music and passing it off as your own?" Tobias asks.

"I don't pretend anything. I've paid my dues. Sampling is an art form. It transforms the meaning of time," Simon fires back.

"Acceptance for you, Simon, is to never accept defeat," Tobias continues, watching as a gaggle of moped riders gather round a Thai takeaway's entrance.

"Who the hell do you think you are?" Simon raises his voice, a group of students eating chips in the seats behind them burst out laughing.

Tobias points at his lapel pin. "There's nothing in a caterpillar that tells you it's going to be a butterfly, Simon."

Simon's eyes are fixated on the two amethysts at the end of the gold pin.

"Consider me a man who wants to help you get where you want to be," says Tobias.

Tobias passes Simon a slim cream envelope. Simon stuffs it angrily into his coat pocket. He jumps off the bus near the Catholic church and heads to the flower shop on the High Street to buy Sonia flowers. Arriving back at the flat, he plans to smoke a spliff.

But Sonia is home already. She has her head turned into the couch. Her top is lifting to the rhythm of her sobbing and Simon sees the bruising on her stomach from the IVF injections is slowly fading.

"How are you feeling?" he says, sitting beside her with the flowers in hand. "Do you want me to get you anything?"

"I have to process this now, before the future can begin."

Simon can't think of the right thing to say. "I got you some ranunculus. The lady at the flower stall told me they were in season again. Do you want me to put them in a vase? I know you like doing that part."

"Just put them down on the counter. And thank you — you're sweet to me."

Simon puts the flowers down and notices a caterpillar crawl out of the bunch toward the stove. He ignores it, returns to the sofa next to Sonia and comforts her. Sonia starts to feel a little better and offers to boil some eggs to have with a salad Simon made yesterday. Simon removes the envelope from his jacket pocket and slides his finger down the seal.

"What's that smell?" Simon says, stepping toward the kitchen and sniffing the air before he's had a chance to see the envelope's contents.

Sonia moves the pan of boiling eggs from the flame and Simon sees the caterpillar is laying on its side burned to a crisp.

"Poor little thing," says Sonia, moving it away from the flame with a teaspoon and putting it in the bin.

Simon's eyes widen as he looks into the envelope. "There's fifteen hundred pounds in fresh fifties in here."

"Wow, who's that from then?" Sonia asks, wiping her cheeks with her sleeve.

"Tobias, a guy from the Rings and Things group."

"What kind of person does that? He must have a motive?" Sonia puts the eggs back on to boil.

"He said he wants to help us. I don't know," replies Simon, slapping the envelope against the palm of his left hand.

Sonia shakes her head. "You don't just take money from strangers without knowing what they want in return. The world doesn't work like that."

"Do you think I should give it back? He suggested we could put it towards the baby." Simon grips the envelope a little harder.

Keeping one hand on her stomach, Sonia takes the envelope from him. "Something doesn't feel right. What else does he know about us?"

"Well, he's been coming to the therapy sessions and they encourage you to open up there. He seems to know about the baby somehow as well," Simon mumbles relieved to finally share his unease with Sonia; too many things hadn't felt right lately.

"Who exactly knows about our IVF?"

"I don't know. It's got to be too much and it's all blending into one thing, ever since I started the group sessions." Simon's eyes shift before resting back on the envelope. He swallows and manages a weak smile as he raises his gaze to take in the squint and pursed lips occupying Sonia's face.

"I love the Happy Service," says Sonia. "But you have to admit, sometimes information does go astray, and maybe it's a mix up, but who gives away that kind of money and in such an unofficial way?" says Sonia. "Do you think we should be concerned?"

"Perhaps. I don't know."

"It's feels risky," says Sonia. "And we'll still need quite a bit more than this. It's a really expensive treatment."

"It's a good start, though. I can sell off my music equipment to pay for the next round — make up the difference," Simon offers without pause.

"How much is your gear worth?" Sonia looks like she's doing complex math in her head.

"About six thousand, maybe seven. We could take a loan to cover the shortfall, if needed, I guess?"

Sonia's sigh followed by a long silence reveals her deep dislike of borrowing.

That night Simon wakes in a cold sweat, imaginary drops of mercury trickling over his skin. In his dreams he'd been flying, and the flash of ancient rivers reflecting the moonlight had been guiding him. The objective was up ahead. Explosions were surrounding him. He goes downstairs for a glass of milk and puts the empty carton in the bin. He notices the caterpillar is still moving. He picks it out, cups it in his hand and places it on the windowsill.

Returning to bed, he wakes in the early morning to an empty bed. He opens his Opalune-sedated eyes and hears groaning: primal sounds reverberating from the hard surface of the bathroom tiling.

He finds Sonia sitting naked in the en suite, her head bowed, arms crumpled onto her legs with her hair down by her shins. A piece of toilet paper lies on the floor next to her. It looks like an imperial Japanese flag, white with a perfect spot of red slowly expanding.

"Is something happening?" Simon asks in trepidation.

"Yes," Sonia replies with a sharp intake of air.

"Is it the..." he stops short of naming the sac with no name.

"Just leave me alone, please," Sonia says with a gasp.

"What can I do?" Simon holds his hands to his head.

"Nothing," Sonia says, raising her voice halfway between talking and shouting.

"Does it hurt bad?" Simon says, though he thinks he should stop asking questions.

"Yes," Sonia says with a hiss.

"Would you like some painkillers, or tea?" says Simon, feeling absolutely useless.

"Just leave me alone," Sonia cries out through the last contraction.

21

It's Their Party and They'll Cry If They Want To

Simon has spent all day transferring his vinyl to a large file WAV format. Sonia has taken a half day off work to recover from the ghost miscarriage.

She has used the rest of the day to squeeze her connections in the human resources department to get Simon a DJ gig for the Four Core Mining annual work party. Everything he once mixed with his hands is now invisible, a collection of zeros and ones on his new MacBook hard drive. The corporate jobs pay well, which is good, because a private doctor in town called Dr Nalbandian is going to need money to deliver them a chance of a test tube baby.

Simon has given up on the studio for the day and is in the kitchen chopping salad. They're having a dinner party, which had been planned before they got the bad news. Sonia hurries to the door to greet their first four guests. She's wearing a long green dress, the hem sweeping the hallway's cream tiling as she welcomes them into the flat. Simon notices she walks more slowly to let the last couple in; the night will be taxing.

The three couples sit waiting to receive Simon's curry chicken; yellow candlelight licks at the wrinkles collected on the faces gathered round a fold-out table set in front of the black marble fireplace of their lounge.

"How are you doing with the takeover, Sonia?" asks their friend Martin, who is slightly over-dressed in a burgundy velour blazer and bow tie, with his hair greased back.

"As usual, all the changes mean I have to do the work of everyone who has left the company, or has been made redundant," replies Sonia.

"For no additional recompense, I wish not to imagine?" Martin says, his eyebrows pinned high like he's auditioning to be Dracula.

Sonia shrugs. "I follow the buses they throw the staff under — tidy up the corporate mess. The problem with marketing in a world led by social media is that everyone thinks they are an expert because they got ten thousand likes for rescuing a goat that got trapped in a fence."

"Sounds pretty shocking," replies Martin, spitting a drop of red wine from his lips on to his pressed white shirt.

Sonia stares at the candle on the table for a moment before continuing. "My last boss left to set up a sausage seasoning app with no prior warning. I did his job for six months before another man was brought in with less experience."

"So stressful," says Martin's wife, Sue, supportively. Her blonde hair is tied up with a polka dot headscarf; it falls to the side as she leans in.

"I don't know if I can make all of this work," says Sonia, stifling the tears welling up, liquid globes reflecting in the light.

The men look at the carpet. The carpet stares back. The women at the table look at Sonia and make nice noises.

"Just remember, it's only work and not really who you are," offers Sep, a powerfully built Italian who used to be Martin and Simon's accountant. His wife, Talia, is as thin as he is wide and works as a hairdresser on the Queens Park's high street. Friends have overused the taxes, death and haircuts joke. It's getting less funny. Time is moving on.

"I can't make good eggs when I'm stressed," Sonia blurts out.

Martin's expression suggests he thinks it's a cooking problem. The conversation is scraping along mental pack ice.

"I think..." says Simon.

"What you think changes nothing," barks Sonia.

"Would you like us to go, Sonia?" offers Talia.

"No, please stay... Really, I'm alright," Sonia replies, looking like she's just sucked all of the remnants of her being back into one jumbled whole.

Everyone sips their drinks, desperate for a natural pause.

"So, exactly what is a sausage seasoning app?" asks Sep through wine-stained teeth.

"Pretty self-explanatory," replies Simon.

"There is a lot of money to be made for the right kind of app, now that the world is psychologically addicted to the smart phone," remarks Martin.

"It's a shame I was thrown out of my computing class in 1983. We were just about to learn Pascal code," says Simon.

"I think our brains missed the boat," remarks Sep, tapping at his wine glass with his manicured index finger.

"At least we lived through the beginning of the capitalist dream, the neon nights, wine bars and the drum machines," adds Martin.

"Speaking of drum machines, mine are going up for sale

tomorrow. Sonia and I are having to pay to have a baby now," says Simon.

"It's an expensive business, I've heard," says Sep, and Talia stares at him hard.

"Simon was given some money by a stranger the other day," says Sonia.

"Tobias isn't a stranger," Simon replies.

"Well, he's not exactly your friend, either." Sonia sits back in her chair and folds her arms.

"He turned up at a tinnitus group I go to every Wednesday," says Simon, slightly embarrassed. "He's a bit strange, wears sandals and a lab coat. But why look a gift horse in the mouth is what I say."

"It's funny, sometimes we refuse to accept that people do nice things for each other and there doesn't have to be any strings attached," says Sep.

"That's not far from what Tobias said in our group, and he got called a hippy," says Simon.

"I was living in a flat in Bristol in the late nineties," says Martin to the room that has fallen silent, "and a hippy and his wife gave me a small, flat Buddha, cut into a dish where the stomach should have been. He said I should put a coin in the belly, and it would bring me riches."

"Did you put the money in then?" asks Simon.

"Yes, I put in as many coins as would fit. I even put a euro in."

"Did anything happen?" Sonia asks.

"Sue got pregnant with Richard, our first," replies Martin with a chuckle.

"Maybe we should get you one of those money Buddhas," Sue offers almost apologetically.

Simon brings the curry over then and the chat dries up as everyone eats in awkward silence.

Within an hour the couple are alone. Simon and Sonia both know their guests have all gone home to pay their babysitters.

22

The Dog Walker
and The Drum Machines

It's a crisp monday morning and Simon has put a listing for his studio drum machines on Gumtree. A man with the handle "JohanVolkmar4" replies almost immediately. Within half an hour the man appears at the door dressed in double denim with a Che Guevara-style soft cap.

"Hi, you must be Johan?" says Simon.

The visitor nods. "Hope you don't mind — I stopped by while walking this lot," he says, indicating a wolfhound, an Alsatian and an English bull terrier. "It's my job. Can I tie them up here?" Johan points to the square of grass and wrought iron fence in front of Simon's building.

"The garden isn't ours," says Simon. "Try the lamp post on the street." Simon points back out to the road.

Johan turns around and ties the three dogs to the lamppost. Then he follows Simon upstairs to the flat. Once they are sat inside the lounge, the dog walker refuses a cup of tea and talks slowly with a deep resonating tone.

"I know some musicians who used to live on this street in one of the bomb houses."

"Bomb houses?"

"Have you not noticed how the rows of Edwardian terraces round here have a few architectural aberrations thrown in between?"

"I can't say I have. But now that you mention it, I guess you're right, they do."

"I used to play in bands with the guys who lived at number 44. They kept all of their instruments under the stairs. There was a fire one night and my keyboard got burned."

"That's terrible," says Simon. "Was everyone OK?"

"We were out in the studio making music. Only the equipment got harmed," Johan explains.

Simon nods. "Lucky!"

"I don't know if you could call it lucky. The guys stole my ideas and cut me out."

"How did that happen?" says Simon, shaking his head.

"So, I was playing volleyball in a park in Duisberg one summer and this kid goes by on a bike, and he has a boom box strapped to it." Johan makes the shape of a big box with his hands.

Simon nods and stands up to check the dogs through the window. They are stood as motionless as a child's stuffed animals.

"And this boy was playing the music I had worked on. There it was, just blasting out," Johan continues in the same lilting, laconic tone.

"It's a great feeling to hear your music out in public being enjoyed by people, especially if you don't know them," adds Simon, aware of the unusual atmosphere developing in the room.

"No, it's not. They stole my music," Johan replies, sounding sad.

"Oh. Sorry. I guess, yeah, if you put it that way," says Simon, slightly off guard.

"And they never paid me for it." Johan looks at Simon dolefully.

"Which act are we talking about again?" Simon asks, out of respect for a fellow artist, rather than actually wanting to know.

"Lots of them. It happened again this week with some other guys I worked with. I walked into a café in Hampstead and three songs that I had written came on the radio while I was sat there reading the paper." Johan carves his hands through the air slowly as he explains.

"What is your name as an artist?" Simon attempts to be supportive.

"DJ Hurricane," Johan replies with a blank look on his face.

"So, you're a DJ and producer then?" says Simon.

"People stole my chords, my bass lines and somebody burned my keyboard under the stairs at number 44," Johan says with a hint of anger muddled up with pride.

"You should get a lawyer and go after them. What are the names of the tracks and who are the people?" Simon asks, choosing an appropriate level of seriousness to wear on his face.

"Garage people. Here in London. Some of it was made at my house and some was in their garage. It was set up as a writing room," Johan explains matter-of-factly.

"So, it was two-step garage made in a garage?" Simon visualizes him in a cold, concrete-floored room with 135 bpm beats rattling off the metal door and two kids making builders tea and skinny spliffs to save on tobacco.

"It was on in a bierkeller too. I've had to stop going to places that have music," Johan says with a sigh.

"Nowadays music's everywhere," Simon adds.

Johan stares out the window wistfully. "All over, I know. It's inescapable."

"OK, do you want to see the gear now?" Simon stands up to lead them out of the melancholy mist musicians specialize in and leads them down the hallway in silence.

Upon entering the studio, Simon sits down and reaches around the back of the chunky wedge of steel, rubber and electronics that forms the Akai sampling drum machine. He turns it on with a muted click and slips a floppy disk into the drive. The machine begins whirring and chomping. A drum break by Mountain arrives sliced up into pieces on the sixteen pads.

Johan punches his index finger into one of the grey rubber pads and the speaker spits out an angry snare. Moving their heads back in unison they avoid the sonic crackle of the audio shrapnel. Johan smiles as he slips his hand into his worn denim jacket and pulls out a block of tattered cash wrapped in rubber bands. The bundles thud gently on top of the Wurlitzer keyboard, hitting the black keys and forming an unusual stabbing chord that lingers in the air.

"I'll give you £8,000 for the Akai drum machine and this keyboard," Johan says, tapping his fingernail on the fiberglass top of the Wurlitzer. "And the EMU drum machine." Johan raises the stakes, looking Simon in the eye.

Simon exhales. "I'd be sad to let that go. They're both good machines."

The chord played on the Wurlitzer is resonating between their words like the long tail on a bad aftershave.

"The Akai is good for programming and the EMU has the dirt and aggression," Simon continues in second-hand sales mode.

"Hmm, programmed aggression. Older technology has more personality, don't you think?" Johan adds, forgetting himself.

"Yes, but it's inconvenient in some ways. I've just got started with the laptop. It's easier but it feels like something's missing," Simon says, pointing at the MacBook folded up on the cane chair next to them.

"My brother Tobias has been looking for a Wurlitzer. I would like to give this one to him," says Johan.

"Is this money from your brother then?" says Simon.

"What difference would that make? Art, Simon. It transcends time, like the people who make it, but only children make us feel that we can live forever."

23

Nerds Are on The Dance Floor

Simon is standing on a stage in a converted barn belonging to the owner of Four Core Mining. The Employee of the Year Awards event is held on the owner's property in Bicester, Oxfordshire, every spring. The DJ equipment is set up at the back of the barn and the smell of large animals hangs in the air. A heavy cotton canvas tent billows out from the open side of the barn. The inside looks like an eighties nightclub, all neon and plastic trees.

Simon has been learning to use his laptop to play music and spends the opening hour of his set staring at the screen with a mild look of fear on his face.

In Simon's peripheral vision, a small man in a blue silk tuxedo climbs the set of stairs at the side of the stage. "Have you got any Sophie Ellis-Bextor?" the man says as he approaches the decks with an ungainly gait.

"Who?" replies Simon, pulling his headphones off to hear him.

"Sophie Ellis-Bextor," repeats the man, swaying slightly.

"Spiller do?" replies Simon, hoping he will leave.

The man forms his hands into fists enthusiastically.

"Agadoo too, yeah, and some Sabbath."

Simon nods, hoping to keep him at bay by staring at the screen of his silver-skinned laptop. The new software is currently flashing fruit-coloured sound waves, like a game of Tetris playing horizontally inside an Excel spreadsheet.

But the man persists. "Did you get my track choice from Vicki?"

"Which one was it?" Simon picks up the printed list he regrets asking the clients to compile. The collection of employee favourites was supposed to make the party easier to navigate; now it's a democracy-driven crap shoot.

"The list from Vicki in events?" Simon says, making sure they're on the same page.

"Yes, the track," the man slurs.

"Which one is yours? There are four hundred songs here. Mixing needs to happen now, I'm sorry."

Simon puts his headphones back on as the numbers man stands there watching.

"I can do this!" he shouts.

"Sorry, I didn't get that," Simon replies politely.

The man pushes his phone toward Simon triumphantly.

"I can do your job if you like? Let me plug in my phone."

"Maybe you can have a go later fella. Everything in its own time."

Don Cheng, the owner of the mining company, has arrived at the decks and Paul suddenly scuttles away. Don is a short, stocky man with a shaved head. He's the only person in the barn wearing a white tuxedo.

"Can you play harder?" Don asks without introducing himself.

Of course, Simon knows who he is. Mr Cheng's soft hand-

110

shake feels like cuts of cold ham against Simon's hot and sweaty DJ fingers.

"What kind of hard?" Simon asks, searching for guidance from the master of all the unlucky people in the room.

"Carnival hard. Slaughter beat," comes the staccato reply, said with such conviction that Simon feels embarrassed to have missed out on an entire genre of music.

"Do you have any song titles?" asks Simon, scared that he'll be sacked on the spot.

"From Carnival — live beats, with sonic boom," the owner instructs, punching his right fist into the palm of his left hand, the red peonies pinned to his white tuxedo lapel shaking with the force of impact.

"But we're in a barn in Bicester," replies Simon to the back of Don Cheng's head, as the king of Four Core Mining makes his way back to a table bedecked with expensive flowers and cotton napkins folded artfully to look like swans.

Simon turns his gaze back to the laptop perched on top of a flimsy metal stand bought from Amazon two days earlier.

Then event organizer Vicki comes rushing from the bar. "You can stop now, Simon. We have our speeches scheduled," she barks in his ear.

With zero subtlety Simon smacks the fader to zero just as Sonia climbs the stairs to say hello. He jumps down from the stage, reaching back to assist Sonia down to the straw dance floor. Together, they head over to the bar at the back of the tent. Sonia takes him by the hand and introduces him to some of the staff that are congregating around a snack table. She asks what Simon would like to drink and heads over to the bar.

"Good job, DJ," a voice shouts to Simon's right. He turns

and it's Johan who bought his drum machines.

"Oh, hi. I wasn't expecting to see you here?" Simon tries to hide his surprise.

"I came with my sister, Allyssa. Her husband works for Four Core."

"I see... How are those machines I sold you doing? Classics, right?"

Johan shakes his head vigorously. "I can't use them."

"Why did you buy them then?" Simon leans in with a shrug.

"To take control of what people did to me in the past," Johan replies with his head back, looking at Simon down his nose.

"Alright, then." Simon feels that trickle of cold winding its way inside of his body again.

He looks over to the bar, where a thickset man in dark green lederhosen is licking beer foam from the tips of his eighteen-inch moustache. Next to the man, Sonia is ordering a round of drinks; she looks upset. Simon bids farewell to Johan and rushes over to be at Sonia's side.

"What's going on?" says Simon.

"The company might be letting me go," Sonia replies, turning her face from Simon's gaze.

"Go where?" he asks as a red laser bounces around the dry ice hanging above them.

Sonia stares through the dance floor into infinity. "It could be over for me at Four Core. I had a chat with a girl called Allyssa while you were DJing. Her husband let it slip that Human Resources are planning a big shake up."

"But you won Employee of the Quarter not so long ago. They can't let you go," says Simon in disgust.

"I guess we'll soon find out," Sonia says, her green eyes glowing in the alternating coloured lights of the work disco.

24

A 38 Percent Chance

Back at home Simon and Sonia sit in silence in their blue unisex nightgowns. It's ten past eleven on a Tuesday morning and they are both unemployed. Sonia got the letter informing her of the restructure on Monday. She decided against interviewing again for her own job. As one of the few people in the office with any principles, she didn't agree with this method of rewarding hard work.

"We don't have enough money, do we?" says Simon, reflecting that all problems, eventually, become financial problems.

"We're about £11,000 short of what we need to get started," replies Sonia.

"I can sell the rest of my vinyl collection." Simon takes his own breath away.

"Are you sure about that?" Sonia asks, eyebrows raised.

"Yes, I am," Simon replies steadfastly.

"I dated a few guys who were always changing their minds before I met you, Simon."

"I know I'm lucky. Most people who meet me think I'm crazy, and most people who fall hard for music tend to have a screw loose."

"The difference with you is that you want to do something about it," says Sonia.

"I do mean it about my records. They won't be hard to sell. The past means very little to me right now," says Simon.

"I appreciate you've made changes, tried to face your demons down."

"At some point, doing something about it becomes one of only two choices. You've seen it when I do nothing. I dread to think what would have happened without you or the insistence of Dr Patel. She was the one who persuaded me to accept that I have to keep taking the drugs, the ones that stole half of my personality and cast it away."

Sonia opens her arms wide. "It's safer like this. Together, we can do this. I promise, Simon. I love you."

"I love you, too," he replies and moves over to hug her on the sofa. The sound of a siren passing the window interrupts their moment.

Simon proceeds carefully. "Will Four Core offer you a decent redundancy package?"

"They probably have two people in the Human Resources department working full-time to prove that they don't need to," Sonia says, as her lip stiffens.

Simon tuts. "That's nice of them."

"It's mining. Men rule the roost. Anything goes if it makes profit."

"I'm sorry," says Simon.

"It should take a couple of months for the money to come through. That's if we get any."

"When can we go again with another treatment of IVF?" Simon asks, rubbing his palm on her tummy gently.

"I have to wait until the effects of the miscarriage have

healed. And... I need some time," Sonia says, staring at the night sky creeping in through the open curtains.

"How long?" Simon whispers.

"A few weeks. We can still go and visit the new doctor. The one your doctor suggested while you were talking to the MacMillan nurse at Charing Cross. I've organized an appointment." Sonia reaches over to the side table and picks up a folded white letter.

"Dr Untermeyer told you we should go here?" says Simon.

"He seemed concerned after he told you about your problem down there."

Simon realizes his sperm production capabilities have yet to be tested after his prostate operation.

"Dr Nalbandian is his name," Sonia says, turning the paper to show a table of results displayed on the back. "It says there's a thirty-eight percent success rate with each round."

"How is his success rate that high?"

"He does things with your blood," Sonia replies flatly.

Simon squints with a shiver. "And it was definitely Untermeyer who told you to see him?"

"Yes, I think that was his name. He seemed to be nice though, didn't he?"

"He was cold, but he did explain everything in an official way."

"He was due to see forty-four patients that day. I remember being struck by the numbers on the wipe board outside his office."

"I need to speak to my mum about the blood thing. She has lots of experience with doctors. It's alarming. I'll see what she has to say."

Simon kisses his wife on the head and leaves her to finish

watching the show. He climbs the stairs to the upstairs bed-room, walks over to the skylight, and calls his mum, Anne.

"They want to do things with Sonia's blood. It's getting scary, Mum."

"If you both want this as much as I think you do, it's worth the risk. I would have done it to have you if I'd had to."

"But I hurt you for good by being born, didn't I?"

"No one knew that rheumatoid arthritis was going to affect me that badly after you were born, Simon," says Anne. "The social services suggested we put you up for adoption. We had to place you with another family for three months when you were one year old. While I recovered, your dad went to work."

"I never knew it was that bad," says Simon. "The wheelchair just became part of the family, a part of who we were. But trying for a baby of our own has got me thinking more about what you went through."

"Life is meant to be hard," says Anne. "Grin and bear it. Good times will come."

"I'm so sorry I hurt you, Mum."

"Don't be sorry. You've brought me so much pleasure, my beautiful son."

"Have you had any luck finding a picture of your father?"

"Your dad is chasing it up with Grandad Jack's squadron but there's been no luck so far. It was a long time ago. We found out fifty-five thousand men died doing that job, and Jack was shot down twice. He survived the first time. My mum bought him a piece of jewellery to welcome him back home. "

"What was Grandad doing exactly?"

"It's all been swept under the carpet, Simon. It's all too sad and only the people who still hurt want to know."

25

And the Board Said Come to Me

It's a sheet grey windy day and Simon and Sonia are walking hand in hand past the Georgian townhouses of Harley Street. The clouds are saturating the earth with a blanket of drizzle as the couple arrives at the panelled blue door of Dr Nalbandian's Pregnancy Assistance Clinic. Simon is nervous to step on such storied ground. This particular part of London has offered expensive answers to bodily problems for over three hundred years. Half of it flies and half of it is quackery.

Simon presses the button that shines like a golden nipple on the brass bell. The door buzzes and the lock clicks open to let them in. The clinic's high-ceilinged hallway welcomes their eyes with row upon row of cheaply mounted photographs of newborns, nailed to the wall like trophies.

Simon and Sonia enter the waiting room to the annoyingly perky sounds of children's daytime TV. The lush blue carpet underfoot hides the footsteps of the childless being shepherded between the rooms. They take a seat together on a brown leather sofa and wait in the stuffy room packed with the needy and biologically unfortunate. Eye contact is minimal. Nobody wants to know each other; infertility grief gathers few friends.

After an hour Sonia's name is called and they are invited up the large Georgian staircase to the doctor's office. With a collective intake of breath, they knock on the door and slope in self-consciously The room has an elaborate corniced ceiling. Behind the doctor's chair an ostentatious white marble fireplace exudes the historical air of unfortunate deeds executed by a distant empire.

The doctor's eyes reflect a weary sense of power mixed with a trance-like boredom. His expensive watch hangs loose from his wrist like a gold snake reclining around willing flesh.

Simon did an internet search before he came: Dr Nal-bandian wears fine silk suits because he makes millions in the baby game. He trades in discoveries that claim to unlock the fallow womb, tricks that tickle the tails of exhausted sperm. He has the highest successful percentage rate, if you believe his methods of calculation, and with this number he has insatiable demand. People want babies like nothing they've wanted before. Every inch of the royal blue carpeted rooms, even the basement, is dedicated to meeting this desire.

"You will need an intravenous immunoglobulin trans-fusion," starts Dr Nalbandian.

"What's that?" Sonia and Simon ask simultaneously.

"Your body is trying to attack itself," says the doctor.

Simon looks hard into his eyes; the doctor returns a hollow factual look and sets his eyes back to his papers.

"But... I," Sonia stumbles.

"You have already miscarried," says the doctor. "Do you want a baby?"

"Yes, of course. That's why we came to you," Sonia tries to explain.

"Next couple, please." The doctor presses an intercom to let the receptionist know he's expecting a new set of dream seekers.

Simon tries to grasp more of his expensive time. "But can you at least tell us what the test involves?"

"Sorry, I have a lot of people to see. Speak with the nurse in reception. She has a regime and protocol already laid out for you," Dr Nalbandian smiles.

The couple exit the gold-trimmed luxury of his office in silence and Simon holds Sonia's hand firmly as they traverse slowly down the baby-lined Georgian staircase. They ask for the nurse at reception and have to queue in the hallway for another half hour. The nurse calls Sonia's name and they pick up a white paper bag filled with bottles of hormones and needles. Sonia pulls out the envelope stuffed with cash from Tobias and hands it to the nurse, who counts it out like a DJ who has just played the main room at a dodgy club. Simon asks himself who this baby is really going to belong to: for a moment it feels like it could be more than just himself and Sonia.

They exit the heavy blue door of the clinic and make their way to the Bakerloo line in the mist of unrelenting drizzle. They board the next tube train to Queens Park and make no effort to communicate over the screeching of the wheels on the tracks.

That night after dinner, Simon watches as Sonia prepares to begin her new hormonal drug regime. She peels her jeans and underwear down to her knees in the lounge and presents herself to him on all fours. All this would normally result in a redirection of blood to Simon's manhood, but it's too clinical and there's a catheter laid inside of him like a plastic skeleton getting in the way. Sonia's backside glows in the flashing light of the muted TV. Simon takes out a chilled bottle of synthesized hormone from the fridge and places an adapter into the sticky concoction, pulling the plunger up in one smooth, steady movement. The viscous transparent liquid fills the barrel to 1.5 millilitres. Simon holds it up to the light, flicks it to release the air bubbles, and attaches the shaft of the needle. He unscrews the plastic protector and the bevel flashes gun-metal grey as he prepares for the next step.

"Are you ready?" he asks Sonia, his voice wavering.

"Yes!" she replies testily.

With an unconvincing thrust, the thick steel needle goes a centimetre into Sonia's flesh, catching against the fibre in her buttock muscles. Simon drops the syringe and the needle falls out of his hand, bouncing against Sonia's backside and pulling her skin up into a lump.

"Come on. Get it over with!" Sonia shouts like a sergeant major bellowing at new recruits.

"I feel funny," Simon says tepidly.

"Think about how I feel," Sonia spits in frustration.

Simon steadies himself like a dart player aiming high for treble top. "OK, I'll try again."

"ARGHHHHHH!" Sonia's animal scream pierces the room as Simon pushes the needle three inches into her right buttock.

The sensation of the needle-point plucking and pinging against her tissue sends him over the edge. "I'm trying but I don't think I can do it," he says. "I'm so sorry, honey."

Simon watches Sonia crawl on all fours from the lounge to the bathroom. Eventually he joins her — just in time to watch her reaching around to take control of the syringe. She squeezes the plunger to its base and pulls it out in a reverse Hari-Kari.

Round three of their treatment begins.

26

The Interview

That night Simon enters a period of REM sleep. Injecting Sonia with egg-plumping hormones has sent a shock wave through his over-sensitive brain, triggering a night terror. In his dream, Simon is crawling along the edge of an aircraft wing shouting "Queenie" at the top of his lungs. His fingers slip off the cold condensation covering the aluminium and he slides off the wing into the inky black night.

The flight to the bottom of the stairs, from their loft bedroom down to the hallway, takes barely a second. Halfway through that solitary moment Simon wakes up to find himself flying upside down. Simon's olfactory nerves register the strong smell of fresh paint on the hallway walls. Then he lands shoulder first in a heap at the bottom.

The bang of flesh on wood wakes Sonia up and she rushes down to find him curled up in a ball cradling his left arm. The journey from sleep to internal injury has created a strange silence between them. Sonia dresses Simon in a nightgown, his body hunched over like a pauper's cadaver ready for the sack. She orders a taxi. It arrives at 5:30 a.m. to take them to the nearest A&E at St Mary's Hospital in Paddington.

Sonia has an interview with a company called Skrape that

same morning at 8 a.m. Fortunately, the company's headquarters are two tube stops from Paddington on the Bakerloo line. She takes the time to pack some makeup and choose a suitable black dress while they wait for the taxi to take them to hospital.

Under the ugly bright lights of a cramped consultancy room, a trainee doctor wraps Simon's wrist with wet plaster and gauze. Simon has fractured his left radius and dislocated his little finger at the first knuckle. Sonia applies her makeup for the interview in the mirror above the hospital sink as the nurse finishes up his plasterwork.

"You look beautiful," manages Simon.

Sonia leans across the paper-covered bed and kisses Simon on the lips. Simon imagines her striding down the emergency ramp of the A&E and walking into the drone of traffic that marks the start of another London day. He's not surprised when she texts him a bit later to say she was offered the job on the spot. His wife is an impressive woman.

Back at home that night Simon uses his functioning arm to order a celebratory takeout meal from Moschino Sushini and they sit to eat prettily presented fish from distant, almost empty seas.

"Well done, honey. I'm so proud of you!" Simon congratulates her speedy return to employment with a raised glass of Asahi beer.

"I think you need to see someone," she returns flatly.

"But I'm already married to you," Simon jokes.

Sonia nods toward his plastered wrist. "It's not a laughing matter — look at the state of you."

"But you just got a job! We should be celebrating!" Simon exalts.

123

"You need to promise me that you'll go and see someone," Sonia says, her voice deepening.

"Like who?" he asks.

"A sleep therapist," Sonia replies curtly.

Simon mouths the words silently before accusing her of the world's most popular sin. "You've been researching it online, haven't you?"

Sonia stares at him. "Promise me."

"Come on! You should be happy. Let's celebrate your new job! How about a glass of wine?"

The room falls silent for a moment.

"I can't have a baby with someone who throws themselves down the stairs, Simon."

"I didn't throw myself... I was climbing across a wing, trying to get away from something." Simon makes invisible ladder climbing movements as he explains.

"Away from what? Me?" Sonia says, exasperated.

"Don't be silly. I love you." Simon moves over to Sonia and embraces her gently. "I was clinging to the wing, an engine was on fire, everything on the ground below was burning."

Sonia stares into his eyes. "Please. See a therapist."

"I already go to one," he replies huffily.

"Who?"

"Liz at the Happy Service."

Sonia puts a hand on his shoulder. "You can't sort your head out with another group of crazy people!"

"I agree. But I had no choice." Simon stares at his feet, rubbing them on the carpet. "Physical pain is easy," he continues after a big breath, then his ego retreats to the village of the sensible. "Look. You're right. I'll go to a hypnotherapist. It's gone beyond just talking with a group of men in a portacabin now."

"Thank you," Sonia replies lovingly.

"I'm sorry."

"Don't be sorry. Just face up to it," she says.

"I don't know what it is I'm trying to face," Simon whispers, staring blankly up at the black night sky as the night lights of an aircraft pass above their bay window.

27

Eye-to-Eye Contact

It's 1 o'clock in the afternoon and the Bakerloo line is ghostly. Crumpled copies of The Metro newspaper lay strewn on every seat.

Simon's wearing a pair of loose-fitting black slacks and a white short-sleeved shirt, with a blazer folded neatly over his plaster cast. He exits the sliding doors of the tube, swaps the loose blazer to his good arm, and uses his plaster cast to shield his hair from the distorting blast of an arriving train. He climbs up the powder blue, art deco station stairs and passes the burgundy blood tiling of the station as he exits.

He types the hypnotherapist's address into the GPS on his phone and walks like a lost tourist through the boulevards lined with Edwardian mansions.

After finding the right house number, he limps up the stone steps of the white stucco building, and presses a buzzer marked Gladness Therapy. Simon takes a seat in the windowless waiting room and picks up a copy of a magazine with Vladimir Putin on the cover. He thumbs through the pages, waiting for the session before him to finish.

A sliding door shoots to the side and a six-foot-five man, wearing a red velour tracksuit, exits the room with a gentle nod to Simon. The man's eyes are puffy and pink, but he looks as if he could be a professional rugby player. Simon waits for a second before standing up straight, exhaling heavily, then stepping forward to knock twice on the thin sliding door.

"Come in," a smoky female voice replies in a plummy accent, rich with education.

Simon slides the door across with his good arm and the crown of a blonde bob greets him. A petite woman in an orange mohair jumper and black jacket is scribbling notes into a book at a furious speed.

"Which seat do you want me in?" Simon asks, feeling simultaneously exposed and ignored.

"Whichever one you feel comfortable with," the woman says. She introduces herself as Allyssa then continues taking notes.

Simon supposes the rugby player's problems were so great they have spilled into his own session time. He chooses the seat furthest away from Allyssa and notices the unusual soft pink shoes on her feet: they have elastic strapping and a satin finish, like pointe ballet shoes.

"Have you undergone hypnotherapy before, Simon?" Allyssa asks, finally raising her head to look at him.

She is far too young to be analysing anyone, thinks Simon. "I once went to a show at the Palladium up North and a hypnotist invited people from the audience to act out his silly requests on stage," he replies with a ready smile, remembering how lowbrow it had all seemed.

"I see." Allyssa pauses. "So, you believe in it then?"

"I had an argument with my wife over whether they were all paid actors," Simon continues to explain, looking up to the ceiling as if to inspire further memory of that evening.

"I thought they were playing along. She thought they were away with the fairies."

"And?"

"My wife won the argument when we realized one of the audience members lived on our street. We both agreed you couldn't get him to do anything for any amount of money. He was an incredibly awful man." Simon cups his hands together.

"OK, I see," Allyssa says with a posh-tinted wince.

"And miserable too," Simon recounts.

"Are you willing to give in to this process?" Allyssa asks him bluntly before they depart into the world of subconscious analysis.

"Well, I am paying. So I would want to get something from it," Simon replies with equal frankness.

"Did you come of your own volition?"

"I am coming because I nearly died," states Simon with the misplaced pride of a victim.

"Please, can you explain what you mean?" Palms out, she opens the imaginary barriers in the space between them. "If you feel comfortable enough."

"I woke up flying upside down through the air and broke my wrist. I'd been dreaming." Simon raises the plaster glowing on his left wrist like a pupae and brings his fingers together to make a constricted fist. The knuckle on his little finger is distended.

"I see."

"Hairline fracture in my wrist and dislocated little finger." Simon taps his right-hand index finger against the hardened plaster engulfing his lower left arm; his nail makes a hollow knocking sound.

128

"Were you learning to fly in the dream?" Allyssa says, beginning to settle in.

"I was crawling along a wing." Simon paws the air like a pathetic tiger.

"I see. Do you know why?" she asks slowly.

"That's what I came here to find out," Simon replies with huffy haste.

"What are the things you are most scared of, Simon?"

"As a kid I feared penguins and sharks."

Allyssa looks at him quizzically. "Penguins can't fly."

"Neither can sharks," Simon replies.

"They're highly adapted to one environment." Allyssa hardens her face to look professional.

"I live in West London, though, not on an iceberg," Simon says firmly.

"Sharks live under the ice, don't they?" she says, drawing him out.

"Leopard seals. They're the problem for penguins," Simon explains, with the help of David Attenborough.

"Who eats the leopard seals?" Allyssa drills away.

"The... sharks," replies Simon.

"Did you say you worked in the music business, Simon?"

"No. Not yet I haven't," Simon replies, slightly off guard that she would guess so accurately.

"Can I ask you to close your eyes?" Allyssa's voice softens.

A protective lid slides over an emotionless black eye and Simon is in a library reading a diving magazine. A shark had mistaken a surfer for a seal, chewed his legs and spat him out. He imagined what it would be like to be killed by mistake.

Simon is under.

28

Session Reflection

"So how did it go with the hypnotist?" Sonia asks from her favoured seat on the sofa.

"I don't know," replies Simon, his lower back resting against the fake marble kitchen counter. He's waiting for their teas to brew before he puts the milk in.

"How can you not know?" says Sonia, unconvinced.

Simon slides his hand across the front of his face to remove any sense of responsibility. "I was under."

"Under what?" says Sonia.

"The hypnotist." Simon rattles the spoon against Sonia's cup, to stir the sugar in.

"Was it that physical?" Sonia's eyes widen.

"I don't know. She started talking to me for a bit. Then we talked about penguins. Next thing I knew, I was back on the bus home," says Simon.

"So, you don't remember any of it?" Sonia shakes her head.

"She did have ballet shoes on. It's about the subconscious. I'm not supposed to know," Simon says, tapping the front of his brow.

Sonia leans forward to take a sip of her sweetened tea. "Is it worth the money?"

"We'll find out tonight. If I don't fly down the stairs again, we'll know it's doing something." Simon moves his cup from his weakened left hand to his stronger right.

"Maybe we should film you at night. Get some kind of way to assess it all." Sonia isn't joking.

"Christ, that's taking it a bit far, isn't it?" Simon pushes himself from his resting place on the counter and heads for his Sunday chair.

"Infrared would do it," Sonia ponders, right hand gripping her chin.

"Have you been receiving training from Mossad at your new place?"

"No, but the new place has made me start to look at everything differently," Sonia says, looking into the fireplace.

"In what way?" Simon sits forward on his seat and accidently turns the TV on with his leg on the remote control. He turns it back off in frustration.

Sonia moves her hands in and out like she is playing a miniature accordion. "You have to acquire all the data to take the clock apart."

"Like an instruction manual?"

"There's more to it than that," she replies with a sigh.

"What exactly are you doing?" Simon asks, while screwing up his face into a ball of confusion.

"Skraping," she replies.

"Sounds like a trip to the dentists," he says with a shiver and a shake of his shoulders.

"It's painless but penetrating."

"What is it?"

"It's a way of finding out everything about everyone through their behaviour online."

29

More Than a Woman

Two muffled voices can be heard through the sliding doors.

"Have you ever thought what it's like to be a woman?" It's the voice of Allyssa, Simon's hypnotherapist.

"Not really," comes the deep male voice.

"Violence is easy, isn't it?" Allyssa asks.

"No, it's wrong. It's scary," the man replies.

"But it's an easy place to get to, once the shackles are off," Allyssa suggests forcefully.

"Maybe," he replies.

"What happens to flowers?" Allyssa keeps the pressure up.

"The petals fall off and they... they fade away," the man replies slowly.

"Do you think what you want is quantifiable in feelings?" Her drill bit is spinning.

"Planning for needs? Only the lucky get to plan for their needs," he replies forlornly.

"Do you think women dress up for men or for other women?" says Allyssa.

"For men," he says.

"When they dress up for men, they are at war with each other then?" she says.

"Competition?" he says.

"Same thing," she says.

"Sexuality is a culture," he says.

The voices are becoming one noise now.

"Is it not more about what's inside?"

"The animal?"

"Yes."

"Animals do the same things."

"Like what?"

"All of it in different but identical ways."

"Why are people obsessed with what other people think of them?"

"What has that got to do with sex?"

"Everything."

Simon is waiting for his next hypnotherapy session, listening to someone else's therapy unfold through cracks in the door. The voices hammer away. It all sounds so selfish, interesting and disgusting. They really should really make sure they close the door and fix the soundproofing.

The session ends and Simon enters the room wearing a half-hearted smile, and smells smoke.

Allyssa slides opens the windowless regulation fire door at the back of the room and waves him in for his second session.

"Have you been smoking in here?" says Simon.

Alyssa blushes an intense red as if she was burning up. "We all have our challenges, our own issues, you know, Simon. No one person is perfect." She won't look at him.

"I know," Simon replies as he takes his seat for the ride.

"None of us lives free of sin, in a vacuum," she adds, looking at him for the first time since he arrived.

"I hope you can give up like I did," Simon offers his support.

"Well done, Simon. Well done."

They sit in silence and Simon smiles. Even though the balance of power is shifting, he's still the one paying.

"So, the penguins," she says.

The massage of Alyssa's tar-infused voice sparkles like a trickle of melting black ice. Simon's gaze slips down to the grey carpeted floor. Her voice pitches down, a feather-light panther padding over weighted keys, arriving in the vocal register of a man.

"The penguin is safe for now, but he has to change. Can you see the caterpillar in his beak?" the deep voice asks in a familiar accent.

Simon can't lift his head. Underneath the desk are a pair of size thirteen feet in grey leather sandals. The ballet shoes are crumpled under the hypnotist's chair. A thin trail of white smoke leads back to the wooden pointe burning bright like magnesium tracer fired up into the night sky.

"Can black and white become yellow?" the deep, distorted voice asks.

Please, someone stop this, Simon thinks, but he can't reply.

"If you are yellow like a butterfly, maybe you can fly," says the voice.

Simon wants Allyssa back but it's too late for that.

On the way back home from the hypnotherapist's office, Simon has a strong urge to call his mother. He still hasn't got that playlist done.

"I miss you, Mum," he tells her from the Overground platform.

"It was a shame you couldn't come home for Grandad

Jack's ceremony. We managed to get the wheelchair in, and your dad lifted me up to put a birthday card from my father to my mother in the place of a photograph. It was for her twenty-ninth birthday — the last one before he died. So at least that's something."

"I'm so sorry you couldn't find a photo, Mum. I bet he was handsome. We would have come, but there's just so much going on."

"I know, love. You have your own lives to lead. But I think of you every day, just so you know."

"I'm sorry again for making you ill."

"Don't be silly, Simon. Sacrifices come easy when you love someone. How's Sonia?"

"We've had some troubles."

"Are you still trying?"

"We're still trying. We're trying everything, Mum."

30

The Remix

Simon has spent the last two weeks crawling around like a crab in cheap sportswear. He's been trying to forget things and live in the present. Unfortunately for him, the present is his problem. Now his phone is ringing, like it does about once a fortnight.

"Hello," Simon answers with his best attempt at happiness.

"Hi, Simon. It's Phillip, Phillip Storey."

The name has a distant familiarity like a publicly listed company on the stock market.

"Ah, yes," says Simon, buying himself some time.

"I have an idea. I'm looking after someone I want you to meet," Phillip explains breezily.

The phrase "looking after" could be a reference to adult day care or music management. They share many similarities and now their pay grades are so close, who's to know? Phillip Storey: it's all coming back to Simon now. Dog Dick records. Of course, they had done business before — production work for a failed act that didn't make the final cut.

"Have you still got the label then, Phillip?"

"Yes, we were absorbed into Universal many moons ago, back when the tide turned," Philip says in a manner so upbeat it makes Simon feel sick.

"Is it coming back in now?" Simon deadpans.

"What?" Philip replies.

"The tide." Simon rolls his eyes, forgetting he's alone.

"Oh, yes. I guess so. It's just the water is not as deep as it used to be. It's still as salty though."

"Always salty, Phillip."

"Look, can you meet me in town this week, Simon? I want you to meet this girl I'm looking after."

Simon can already feel an urge to get out of the proposition. "What do you want me to do exactly. Can't you look after her yourself?"

"We can talk a bit more. I was looking at a remix or maybe a production."

A silence hangs after Phillip's suggestion.

"I'm not prepared to spend a week worrying about snare sounds for you to end up turning it down," Simon explains with a groan.

"I won't turn it down," counters Phillip, using his industry-sharpened, hard to pin down charm.

"How do you know? Only a fool would bet on the outcome of creative endeavours." Simon laughs a little too convincingly.

"I have faith in you. And you'll get £200 regardless of what happens."

Two days later, Simon walks to Queens Park tube station, with plans to meet Phillip in a popular Soho basement sushi bar. He's braved some loose jeans and if he can stay sat down behind the cover of a table, no one will know about his catheter. Three chefs carve fish flesh behind glass as Simon positions himself on a bar chair at the end of a long pine table. The restaurant is packed with customers ramming mini fillets into their faces.

Phillip arrives looking just as Simon remembered him. Rakish, with a soft plum jumper clinging to his slim chest, the V in the wool ready to clamp onto his turkey-skin neck. His hair is slicked back, the black and grey matching his Vans deck shoes. He's brought with him a small blonde girl dressed in a Panda onesie; her feet trapped in a pair of eighteen-hole Doc Martin boots, which are squeezing her shins like lamb shanks ready for the oven. She has a china white brittle face, thin nose and an unusual spiky chin. Black eyeliner wraps around her dull grey eyes like crayon dripping down a hot winter radiator.

"Hi, Simon! This is Peski. Peski, meet Simon."

The teenager looks at Simon with studied disinterest. Phillip orders a boat full of sushi and a round of drinks from a passing waitress. Simon clutches at the pint delivered in a tall, thin pilsner glass. Peski and Phillip share some sake from a midget teapot.

"Do you know what Simon has done?" Phillip begins.

"No, come on then. What has Simon done, Phillip?" Peski replies with an unusual pickled arrogance.

"She doesn't need to know about the past," says Simon. "Its old news, Phil."

"Lacer, Bandwidth, Olmecc, Tradbury, the list goes on." Phillip reels the band names off with a sense of borrowed triumph and the words hang in the ether like a failed joke.

"Which list?" asks Peski, nonplussed.

"The list of hit remixes undertaken and delivered by our man with a plan, Simon here." Phillip opens his palms toward him.

"I can see where he is," she replies.

Simon tries to ease the spotlight away from her response. "You aren't bothered about the past and you shouldn't be —

unless you're borrowing from it to make good of the future, that is."

"I'm not hungry." Peski stands up and goes to leave. "I'll let you old men discuss what it is you brought me here for today. I have Insta posts to plan."

"Nice girl," says Simon, with a knowing smile.

"I'm sorry, Simon. You know how artists can be," Phillip pleads.

"Tragic spirit travellers blighted by greed and self-importance, carefully hidden under passive aggressive sensitivity." Simon can't help spoiling Phillip's attempts at a Top of the Pops party.

Phillip sighs. "She's certainly very selfish from time to time."

"So why do you want her to be remixed by me?" asks Simon as he shifts the catheter tap with his plastered wrist under the table.

"I don't know. I've just got a feeling," Phillip explains, sucking air through his teeth.

"You're offering me £200, regardless of the outcome?"

"Yes," says Phillip, fiddling with the tiny sake pot.

Simon lays his worn cards on the table. "I want half the publishing on my version."

"Jesus, that's unheard of," cries Phillip, tossing his head back.

"No, it isn't. It's quite common nowadays. You said you had a feeling, so you can back my side of the deal. Are you really her management? Or are you just 'looking after her'?" Simon turns the screw into the plaster-board wall of silence.

"Let me get you the parts for the song then we can go from there." Phillip dodges the directness.

"Two hundred quid and fifty-fifty or I'm out," repeats Simon.

They shake on it and Philip stands up to take his Harrington coat from the back of his stool.

Simon pretends he is waiting for someone else as an excuse to remain seated and hide his catheter. He says goodbye to Philip, gives it five minutes, then takes his cowboy legs up to Regents Street to catch the number 6 bus home.

Simon looks up at Anteros, the god of returned love, staring down from the Shaftesbury Memorial Fountain, his brass wings steadying the bow, the arrow aimed directly at the bus stop. Hopping onto the first number 6 that arrives, he thanks the driver for waiting, takes his time to present his Oyster card, and heads for the front seats at the top of the stairs. The bus lurches forward and Simon grips the rails in front of him. All around him cream Portland stone clads the Georgian architecture. Liberty's, Hamleys, Jaeger and the Apple store pass the window. Their interiors are lit up cosy and warm to loosen passing wallets.

Pulling up at the next stop, the top deck of the bus looks down into the first floor of the upstairs bar of the Queen's Head public house. Simon sees the carpet is dark red, like abattoir blood. The furniture is carved from burned black hardwood and has a velvet finish. The dimly lit space is empty save for a group of five people who congregate around a table populated with half-finished drinks and a pile of open files. Someone in the group tells a joke and they laugh heartily. As their heads are thrown back in joint mirth, the bus begins to pull away and Simon recognizes them all.

Tobias, Dr Untermeyer, Allyssa, the anaesthetist Dr Frau Brandt, and Mr Bellway, the balding Kiwi sperm-collector, are out having a drink together. Simon's smile doesn't last long as he stares at his reflection floating in the night air before him, every follicle in his body turns cold and the hairs on his fingers stick up like one hundred little keratin soldiers standing to attention.

31

In This Together

Simon arrives back at the flat panting, having walked from the Catholic church bus stop as fast as his catheter allowed him. The hour journey on the bus felt like a dream, his mind trapped, whirring on a hamster wheel of paranoia.

"Tobias knows Untermeyer and Allyssa. Frau Brandt knows that bald guy at the andrology unit and Liz at Rings and Things," Simon rattles off in desperation. "They all know each other privately as well as professionally, Sonia. What the hell is going on?"

"Calm down, Simon," says Sonia, trying to stop his blanc-mange from collapsing. "So what if they know each other?"

"Did you know that they knew each other?" says Simon, pointing back toward the door as if he might have been followed.

"No! Of course not! Maybe they just hang out because they're in a club, like a sailing club, or table tennis or something," she pushes back.

"You're in this with them, aren't you?" Simon takes a two-footed jump.

"You are ridiculous. Have you stopped taking your medication again?" Sonia asks.

"Can you Skrape them for me at work? Use the software to

find all the extra connections?" Simon's hands shake as he tries to batten down his thoughts.

"You're being paranoid. This won't help your healing," Sonia's voice switches to a motherly tone.

"It doesn't add up." Simon has moved to the middle of the lounge bay window. He stares into the black ocean of sky suffocating the spire of the Catholic church, its point illuminated by the orange glow of the streetlamp.

"Look, I can run the software on them if you really want," says Sonia. "Just give me a list of their full names. If you believe in six degrees of separation you should know we're all connected in some form anyway."

Simon feels her eyes boring into the back of his head as his eyes stay focused on the well of blackness clinging to the spire. "They want something from us," he says.

"Like what?"

"They want our baby."

"What do you mean, Simon? Come on! You can't let yourself lose control of reality this way. You've worked so hard to get this far, to be functioning again."

"Someone wanted to take me when I was a baby. They put me with another family because my mum couldn't walk. It was me that triggered her arthritis, then they put her in a hospice. I spent three months with a different family."

"You've never told me that before."

"I need to go up north and see my mother. I feel like I've been letting her down. We've been so absorbed with the treatment. It feels out of control. I would have gone on my own for her dad's ceremony, but I didn't want her to see me like this. I'll go once this cast is off — and the catheter's gone." Simon's other worry resurfaces like a buoy at slack water.

"Of course you should go and see your mum," Sonia says, reaching for his shaking hand. "How is she doing?"

"Mum never tells me straight over the phone." Simon's eyes return to the bright light of the room. "She's protecting me, and I didn't want to worry her with our concerns."

Sonia shifts in her seat. "But we're trying for a baby. Surely she would want to know the ins and outs?"

"Think about how we've felt through the IVF," Simon interjects with a stare. "Imagine if that was your daughter or your son. She knows we're trying. I just don't want to fill her with worry."

"Talking about feelings in an imaginary future isn't going to help. Any parent would want to know. They might be about to become grandparents, after all," Sonia replies, sounding frustrated.

"Worry is best dished out on a need-to-know basis, especially when the person receiving it has been ill themselves." Simon strokes his jaw, the lounge light penetrating easily to the widening crown of his scalp, Grandfather Jack's trait for baldness slowly setting in.

The next morning Simon receives a letter in the post from Dr Untermeyer's office, scheduling a time for his catheter removal. Once he gets his cast cut from his arm, he will be free of the signs of his own physical frailty and ready to go back home and check on his mother.

The next Monday, Simon takes the tube to Hammersmith and limps up the Fulham Palace Road. After navigating the revolving doors of Charing Cross Hospital, he takes the lift up three floors and heads to the south wing. Inside the urology department waiting room he sits in the familiar row of grey seats. Eventually he is called to sit on a red chair inside Dr Untermeyer's office.

A voluptuous assistant nurse with purple nail varnish, radiant dark skin and a pumpkin round face walks in through the white door and, without introducing herself, asks him to take his pants down and lie on the bed. Simon obliges, slipping his yellow MC Hammer pants down until they are crumpled over his white trainers. He sits his milk white, naked cheeks on the hygiene paper and rolls his naked lower half on to the bed apologetically.

The nurse approaches the bed with her big brown eyes fixated on his half man, half plastic equipment. In silence she picks up the tip of his catheter and pulls on a small plastic leaver underneath the body of the valve. Inside Simon, a plastic bubble keeping the borrowed pipework in place deflates.

The nurse turns to him. "Are you ready?" she asks with a stunning smile.

"I need to speak to Dr Untermeyer," Simon says, his brow sparkling with fine droplets excreted in a hot flush of fear.

"I'm going to pull now, Mr Radcliffe. I can ask him once we're all done."

The nurse grips the catheter pipe and makes a whipping motion up away from the bed. The fake urethra Simon has worn deep inside him for six weeks follows her arm up and away. Simon's heart rate slows as his body retrieves all the blood from his capillaries, sending it to his essential organs. His face turns a shade of elephant skin. The nurse drops the catheter into a shiny kidney-shaped tin and Simon starts to drift away. He looks at the floor and rooftops come hurtling towards him just like in his dreams. Anxiety rips him out of his passed out state and for a second his left arm is a giant butterfly wing, resplendent, glowing orange, licked with flame.

When he fully gathers his senses, the nurse has disappeared. Simon finds himself wrapped up in a silk blanket. Dr Untermeyer is towering over his half-naked body. The skin of the doctor's bald head reflects like a varnished egg in the strip lights. The doctor raises his hand to his breast pocket and takes a gold pen from his bright white lab coat.

"That wasn't too bad now, was it?" the doctor says.

Simon feels nauseous, the white room throbs in time, thudding in slow motion bradycardia.

"What do you want from me, Dr Untermeyer?" Simon whispers pathetically.

"Relax, Mr Radcliffe. Now, do you mind if I call you Simon?"

"Are you all trying to help me?" Simon asks, sounding weak and disorientated. "Or hurt me?"

"Now, Simon, we're going to have to see if your equipment still works as it should. Can you promise me you'll test it's functionality as soon as possible?" Dr Untermeyer's voice sounds crisp, wrapped up in his distant bedside manner. "You do know what I mean?"

Simon finds it difficult to look him in the eye. Another man's concern for his ability to masturbate to conclusion is rather unsettling him. "Why is this happening?" he asks, close to tears.

"Ask your mother about Homberg, Simon. She will help you find the way."

Dr Untermeyer turns and moves over to the sink. He leans over to take notes, next to the catheter sitting on the drainage board. The nurse returns to offer Simon a prescription for painkillers and Dr Untermeyer disappears behind her back with a speedy, "Goodbye, my friend."

"I think they want to steal something from me, hurt my family," says Simon to the nurse as she helps him off the bed.

"Get lots of rest, Mr Radcliffe. And drink plenty of water. Can you promise me? Then you will be OK."

32

Long Train Running

Sonia cuts the cast from Simon's freckled left wrist with a pair of gardening secateurs. The remnants of the cast fall from his wrist with a dull clunk, breaking apart in the kitchen sink like an albino lobster moulting. It's a procedure that should have been undertaken with the appropriate equipment in Paddington hospital's outpatients' department. But Simon is sick of the sight of revolving doors and the smell of Costa coffee mixed in with bleach. Now, with his catheter removed and his cast off, Simon can finally walk smoothly. He's feeling less of a physical wreck.

In the morning it will be time to go home, back up north, where the people are warm, and the weather is cold.

Simon takes an early East Coast train from Kings Cross to Newcastle Central Station. A hundred-pound ticket sometimes gets you a piece of floor outside the toilet. He boards at the first carriage and sits in first class, waiting to be asked to leave for his pre-booked economy seat. But the cramped train has trapped the ticket collector behind the snack trolley, just as Simon had hoped. The train pulls from the station and he rides for four hours as if he didn't have to care about money.

Even though his lilac shirt hugs his torso a little too close for comfort, he's wearing it because it's his mother's favourite colour. With it, he's wearing dark blue formal trousers to look smart for the homecoming.

The train offers a fleeting view of Durham Cathedral's gothic form but then it slows down, trundling over the timeless dirt brown of the tidal River Tyne. Simon soaks up the view of Newcastle, from castle keeps to the faded dysfunction of T. Dan Smith's attempted Brasilia. This hardened place once ruled the world through engineering and, in turn, took Simon's heart by function of birth. The old bridges stand firm on the riverbanks. The mist gathers ghosts of the Vikings, the Romans, the coal ships, the machine guns and tanks.

The glory of the Victorian station's arches catch the echo of unknowable voices as the train doors open with a pneumatic groan. The clank of metal pierces through shouted greetings, personal pieces of time trapped for a moment under the high glass ceilings.

Simon's parents are waiting to meet him under the grand sandstone arches. His mother, Anne, greets him in a grey Happy Service wheelchair. She's wearing a thick purple coat with a sparkling brooch made of black and blood red crystals formed into a flower. The brooch bristles with the life force beaming from her. Whatever life had dealt her, that flame had always burned strong. His father, Peter, stands tall in a grey blazer, his chest inflated, fully in control of his feelings and the four wheels that support the chair. A mutual need for a missing parent had bonded the couple. Peter's mother died of tuberculosis when he was five and all he can remember is the stripes on her pinny; Anne was three when the smart man came to the door with a telegram to say her daddy was no more.

Simon bends over to hug his mother and she kisses him

149

on the lips, not his cheek as usual, and it triggers a memory captured on a Kodachrome slide. Simon is six months old, being held in the air and kissed by Anne as she lies on the orange nylon lounge carpet of their New Town home. The one-inch square pieces of his childhood are kept in a plastic box, hidden under nineteen-forties press cuttings behind the lounge sideboard door.

Simon hangs his smaller bag on the back of his mother's wheelchair. The wind outside the station is icy, funnelled up the river from the North Sea and running heartlessly cold. They make their way to the car park next to the multi-coloured letters of the children's Life Centre, arriving at the doors of Peter's low-slung burgundy Ford Orion. The wheelchair is dismantled, the hand rims and spokes whistle in the wind. Simon finishes loading the parts into the boot while Peter guides Anne in. His father starts the engine, and they all sink back into the grey worn seats. Floating on the soft suspension, they drive eight miles north, past the airport, to the bungalow of family dreams.

The road on the approach to the house has fissured cracks from curb to curb, where skateboard wheels would roll. The tarmac was butter smooth back when Simon was a kid; now it's all broken and worn. Anne waits in the car on the drive, smiling contentedly while Peter lifts the folded wheelchair from the boot and remakes it all in working order next to the car. Simon exits the car to help. He stops to spread his fingers out over the passenger window's surface, pushing his palm flat against the cold, shatter-proof glass. Anne meets his hand with hers on the other side and they smile.

After opening the door, Simon positions himself to pick her

up in one movement. He applies the upward pressure under Anne's legs and around her back. Anne purses her lips. It won't take as much strength as Simon expected; his mother is getting lighter now.

He lowers her slowly into the black nylon seat held in the chrome frame. Bending down, he pulls the footrests out by the front rigging, lifts her lilac-trimmed trainers by the soles, and places her feet in the footrests with care. Straightening his back to take the push handles, he leans forward to push the chair and feels the weakness in his left hand from the night leap down the stairs. At the step that leads to the door, Peter takes the wheelchair by the metal skirt and together they lift the woman they love over the threshold into the narrow hallway.

Simon lived in this Dutch bungalow from the age of 12 to 18: from a skinny boy to a half-cocked man. The hallway is dark, enclosed by thoughtless nineteen-thirties architecture. Peter turns on the two side lights over the radiator shelf, revealing the wooden duck leading three painted ducklings toward the kitchen.

Peter has recently taken to collecting wind-up mantle clocks and got a little too good at catching his mechanical prey. The dark wood and marble time pieces are mounted everywhere. Tick-tock trophies in brown and black clutter the shelves, sideboards and floor, their insides opened up and left on trays. Simon's father claims that if he controls time, he will make more money out of his pension and beat the government at its own game — a joke that only he finds funny, but Simon laughs along all the same.

The lounge sports the same décor as the day Simon left. His parents never felt the need to impress anyone.

"Your father's been drinking balsamic vinegar from the bottom of his plate when we've had a salad," Anne says out of the blue with a giggle, propped up by the salmon-coloured cushions on the floral print family sofa, which is by the window and the combination home stereo.

"It's amazing stuff, isn't it? Where did they hide that all of our lives?" Simon says. It was he who had introduced them to the joys of Modena.

"Mostly in Italy, son," Peter replies, looking at his son with a playful smile.

"I wonder if they had any balsamic vinegar imported to use on their burdock leaves when they were building Hadrian's Wall?" Simon says.

Anne's laugh is interrupted by whirring sounds. Clicks and ticks tell of steel springs under duress: an older version of time, hidden behind the face and stored in wound up metal.

It's soon to be 3:57 p.m. The first of the fast clocks is about to blow. For the following five minutes a cacophony of chimes attack from behind the curtains and across the thick pastel rug on the carpeted floor. Tuned steel is struck with vibrating chime rods in a myriad of frequencies. Simon looks at his mother dressed in a pink robe. She is shaking her head at the imposition of the hoarded collection. No one dares speak over the dominant sound, spilling like a flock of ravens gathered and cawing in the late autumn. Peter sits there twiddling his thumbs beneath the tall lamp above his end of the sofa, caught somewhere between embarrassment and boyish pride.

Overwhelmed by a sudden urge to cry, Simon leaves the room and bows his head over the kitchen sink. Resting his brow on his arms he takes a deep breath; his left wrist still smells of yesterday's plaster, split in half and thrown away.

Finally, the chiming clocks stop. Simon pushes his rising emotion back down with a swallow and re-enters the lounge. Peter is standing by the walnut sideboard with his index finger looping through the brass fitting of the cabinet door handle.

"Your dad has found some paper clippings about your grandad," Anne says.

The magnet on the door clicks as Peter pulls it open.

"Jack or Thomas?" says Simon.

"Jack," Anne replies.

"Your mum didn't get a chance to know him, son. She was too young when it happened," Peter says as he turns over a yellowed copy of the *Daily Mail*, the edge of the paper disintegrating, tearing off in his hand.

Simon reads the headline: *THOUSAND BOMBER RAID*.

The following morning they visit the Hancock museum on the Great North Road. It's a sandstone building dedicated to natural history and civilization. Peter parks the Orion in the disabled bays right outside the grand stone entrance. Once Anne is inside the wheelchair, they weave back and forth up the access ramp into the entrance of the museum, where the dinosaurs meet stuffed penguins. In the centre of the main display hall, a scaled version of Hadrian's Wall wiggles its way from the west to the east coast, like a brick centipede crawling over a mould of Cumbria and Northumberland.

"No mention of balsamic vinegar here, son," Peter informs them after reading the panel at the front of the glass-covered display, and the family's gentle laughter echoes up two stories into the vaults of the atrium ceiling.

They stop for a cup of tea in the café, finishing off a round of scones with cream and jam.

"I have something to show you," Peter says, leading them to the back of the café's seating area, where the pale blue wall is filled with row upon row of painted butterflies.

The middle of each insect bears a printed name across its thorax. In the bottom right, a run of Radcliffes are stacked. Anne's name is printed on a purple hairstreak butterfly; two stunning shocks of lilac span the centre of the insect's wings. Peter tells them how he made a contribution to have the name of every living member of the family printed on a butterfly on the wall of the museum.

Anne surveys the display with a gasp and turns to Simon. "My cancer, it's come back, son," she says, squinting as the light from the atrium catches her eyes.

"OK," is all Simon can muster, his guts churning as he moves the wheelchair into the shade to stop his mother squinting. It was a funny time to notice what beautiful green eyes she has.

"I want to visit my father," Anne states with steely determination.

"Where can we find him?" Simon asks, squeezing her hand.

"Reichswald cemetery. We'll be the first to visit him," Anne says, staring at the butterflies as she reads the families names: her sister Pat and brother Alan; Peter's sisters, Joan and Kate, and their many cousins spread out across the wall.

Simon wants to ask his mum about Homberg, like Dr Untermeyer had advised, but his head is spinning too hard. "How long have we got?" he says.

"It's in my lymph nodes now."

That night, Simon lies on his childhood bed in the dark, waiting for the Opalune to kick in. The roar of aircraft engines passes overhead, masking his tinnitus and clawing away at the walls he has built within.

33

Curtains & Infrared

The next morning Simon takes his pre-booked seat in the quiet carriage of the 10:05 train to Kings Cross. Peter is pushing Anne in the wheelchair on the platform alongside the train as it picks up speed to leave Newcastle Central Station; he can't keep up and Simon's parents disappear in the last carriage window. Simon bows his head and places it against the back of the chair in front of him. He wraps his arms around his chest. Turning his head to the side, he catches the bridges of the Tyne straddling the divide soon to be between them.

The train powers through Yorkshire via Doncaster and Peterborough. Each time the train stops the accents of the passengers change, and hot breath meets the cold air on the open platform of places he's never been. As the train departs Stevenage, Simon receives an email on his phone. The subject reads *Peski Parts*. It's from Phillip Storey.

Hi Simon
Great to see you again after all these years! I've included a link to the stem parts for that Peski remix we talked about. The accounts department have given me the go ahead to pay you the £200 upfront. The track runs at 108 bpm. It's all

pretty self-explanatory. Any questions give me a shout. Very excited to hear what you do with it!

Word Up
Phillip

"Word up," mouths Simon, screwing up his face at the cultural misappropriation. Who on earth does Phillip think he is? The Basildon Larry Blackmon? Simon sighs as the graffiti begins to slide by, like 2D fruit lining the blackened Victorian walls of the capital's commuter belt stations. The brakes of the train kick in and the smell of asbestos fibre fills the carriage as Arsenal Football Club's Emirates Stadium passes in the afternoon silence. For a brief moment Simon remembers cold November Saturdays, the steam of twenty thousand men, stale beer, Keegan burgers and the working-class need for agitation. Everything is clean now, graded through shopping mall filters, glassy, fake, unreal, never stained.

He takes the tube from Kings Cross, swaps the Northern line for the Bakerloo, and strides across the chilly mist of Queens Park. Back home their flat feels dark and empty. Sonia is still at work. He puts the kettle on and vows to banish the gloom by putting himself to work on the Peski remix.

In his studio, Simon sits on the light-damaged fake leather of his office swivel chair and opens up his laptop. Under his sock-covered feet the Turkish rug feels soft and forgiving. Around him slabs of vinyl are packed tight on the shelves in sturdy silence. The matt black finish of Simon's record deck sits collecting dust by his side and the smell of Near Mint vinyl cleaner hangs in the air.

Simon opens up his email and clicks on the WeTransfer link

sent by Phillip. Binary numbers arrive in a deluge as invisible music is passed through the Wi-Fi signal.

The individual vocal parts from Peski's track reform as WAV files in a desktop folder. A ping signals the download is complete and the sound triggers a light bulb moment in the music management department of Simon's brain. He remembers that his demo of Peter Gabriel's "Family Snapshot" is also 108 beats per minute. If he can fuse the Peski track with his demo, he'll be reducing his workload in a magical act of technological laziness. Simon finds the session and opens it up. His new software mounts the plugins that succeed in mirroring the hardware of the past and the screen is filled with the grey tones of the digital audio workstation.

LOGIC PRO X SESSION LAST UPDATED NOV 20 AT 19:44
SESSION SIZE 1.2GB
    Track 1 PETER GABRIEL PIANO CHOPS
    Track 2 FAIRUZ VOCAL LOOP
    Track 3 CHERNOBYL STRINGS
    Track 4 LALE ANDERSON DRUM LOOP
    Track 5 HARD KICK
    Track 6 SOFT KICK
    Track 7 HARD HAT
    Track 8 SOUL SHAKER
    Track 9 DRUMMER BOY SNARE
    Track 10 SKY PAD
    Track 11 SILKWORM SYNTHESIZER
    Track 12 BODY PART
    Track 13 BLACK MOON
    Track 14 PETER GABRIEL FRETLESS BASS CHOPS
SWING SETTING 68%

He drags the WAV file marked "vocal lead" over his desktop into the Logic session and places it into a new audio track in the "Family Snapshot" session.

"Raining Down" is the name of the song he's remixing. The original version of the song is dark and spacey: an empty futuristic ballad in D minor. Euro synths melt down over a trickle of picked guitars. The feel of the song switches from a melancholy verse caught out in the cold to a menacing chorus that explodes into action, with power chords punching out holes in the studio air made stale by hot electronic equipment. A Scandinavian metal guitar solo reigns supreme in the outro.

Peski must be sick in the head, thinks Simon, remembering her pale brittle face in the sushi house.

The first line falls on the first beat of the bar. Simon zooms in on the audio to edit the start point right on the nose of the hard letter D. He moves the vocal audio to the first beat of the "Family Snapshot" demo and presses play.

In stunning serendipity, the vocal and the demo are in tune with each other. His brain releases good chemicals — serotonin powers through his synapses. The lyrics unfold in perfect rhythmical positioning, dripping like syrup over the chopped pianos stolen from Gabriel's track.

"Don't tie me up in misconceptions.
Didn't mean to hurt you all the same.
Only following instructions
The tit for tat is just a game
Wrapped in silk you stopped me falling
Find us all some forgiveness, now let us pray."

Peski's icy voice fills the studio room, breathing life into proceedings. The remix is sounding strong. It sounds... amazing! How versions are like lifetimes: choices and opportunities that make us feel we can have things our way.

Simon starts to work on the sonics of the mix, dialling it in closer to a professional production. He's lost in musical manipulation, driven by audio creation, rhythmical mathematics get twisted into equations as he builds the interlocking blocks up into functioning arrangements.

"Hi!" Sonia says, opening the door, and Simon jumps out of his skin.

"Jesus! You nearly gave me a heart attack." Simon kicks his feet into the rug, pushes himself away from the musical furnace. He stops the track with a tap of the space bar on the laptop. He spins his chair around to face Sonia and notices she's carrying a bag.

"What's that then?" he asks, tapping his finger against the box in the bag, as Sonia leans down to kiss him on the lips.

"An infrared camera," replies Sonia nonchalantly, as if she bought one every week.

Simon sighs, feeling trapped. "Oh, God. Here we go."

"How was your mum?" says Sonia.

"Time, it's moving. Bad things are coming back again." Simon slowly stumbles through the words, his lips quivering until he sucks it up and keeps it in.

Sonia sits on his lap in the office chair and her weight disengages the pneumatic cylinder; they both sink with a slow hiss. "Are you going to see her again soon?" she asks, stroking his hair.

Simon stares at the laptop screen — now a sleeping black

mirror reflecting back at them. "She told me she wants to go to Reichswald, to see her father before it's too late."

"Where's that?"

"It's near the Dutch border, around Nijmegen, but on the German side." Simon looked it up on his phone during the train ride home from Newcastle.

"I think that's a lovely idea. It'll be special to help her find some peace within, before... I'm sorry, honey."

"No one from the family has ever been to visit him."

"It should be a great trip then!" Sonia holds the infrared camera in its box with one hand and runs her fingers along the contents listed on the side. "You know we can use this camera for the baby when it arrives, as well as recording your sleep. We can attach it to our bedroom wall easily. It comes with the Rawl plugs, screws and everything."

"That's great," Simon manages to reply, his forced smile ebbing away.

"I can set it to record, or set off an alarm, if you head toward the stairs again," Sonia says.

Simon can tell she feels proud of her plan and wishes he felt the same. "Alright," is all he can muster, despite knowing the benefits of what filming might reveal.

Something about his experiences with Allyssa fills him with a sense of dread. In particular, the deep voice he heard whilst he was under hypnosis. The voice which talked about caterpillars.

Sonia leaves the studio to make them both a cup of tea. She returns five minutes later, placing Simon's cup on the studio worktable. For a moment, Sonia pauses behind Simon to watch him at work.

Simon presses the spacebar and the sweet alchemy of the Peski remix lights up the back of their flat.

"Sounding good!" Sonia shouts over the sound of the drum buss as he ramps up the compression, then she leaves to set up the camera.

Simon ignores the sound of drilling as he finesses the remix. Soon it will be ready to send to Phillip but there are other issues to resolve first — agreements to discuss and contracts to bend to his will.

Over a dinner of salmon fillets with microwaved rice and salad, Simon reveals something else is still playing on his mind.

"How's work going?" he begins.

"It's very political. I'm not sure what we're doing is legal," Sonia says, shrugging.

"What do you mean?" Simon spits a piece of rice across the table as he hits the 'd' in do.

"Skraping means taking something away," Sonia says, biting at her top lip. "They should really call it stealing."

Simon pours himself a glass of red wine. "Did you manage to get the software home on that old laptop?"

"Yes, I've copied it over from my work computer, and I've isolated it so no one can see what it has running on there," says Sonia, smiling.

"Can we put the names in now then?"

"I can, but you have to promise me something." Sonia stops his hand from raising the wine to his lips.

Simon takes her hand with his weak left and holds it.

"Promise you what?"

"That whatever it is, you won't use it for anything in ill will." Sonia squeezes his hand, hurting his swollen knuckle.

"Ow, what do you mean? It's the doctors who've been messing with me!" He pulls his weakened left hand away.

"It looks to me like they saved your life. Promise, Simon."

"OK. I promise. But, after dinner, lets Skrape them all and find out what it is they're doing."

Simon waits until Sonia swallows the last mouthful of her dinner then he goes over to the sofa and picks up her old laptop. He hands it to her at the dinner table. On a green Post-It he writes out the names:

Tobias Volkmar
Dr Untermeyer
Dr Frau Brandt
Allyssa Selwyn
Old balding, ginger sperm collector, Queen Charlotte's and Chelsea andrology unit. Bell something. Add Ake Kaha in.

Sonia looks at the list. "This last one, that's not even a name. You can't expect me to find him."

"I bet you can. There's not many ginger balding men in andrology working in Shepherds Bush."

"You're right! I've found him already," she says, tapping away at her keyboard. "Bill Bellway."

"Told you he'd be in there," says Simon.

"OK, so they're all German, apart from Bill, who was born in Auckland," Sonia says. "And *Ake Ake Kia Kaha* is a saying meaning 'Be forever strong'. It's on the crest of some badge of the 75 New Zealand Squadron."

"That's the same squadron as my grandad, I think. Why do you think they all went out for a drink together?"

"Well, in a way they're colleagues, aren't they?" says Sonia.

"They work in the same field."

"Prostate cancer has nothing to do with IVF."

"Bill Bellway would probably beg to differ."

"OK, so what does the Skrape software say?" Simon asks.

"Three of them are linked by country of birth and four of them are linked by one city," Sonia replies.

"In what way?"

"Four of them have grandparents who were born in Homberg."

In bed that night they talk about baby names. Jack, James, Thomas, Olivia, Christine, and Jane. Soon they will be triggering Sonia's eggs again, making up more than just names.

Simon has a restless night with heavy bouts of sleep talking that wake Sonia. "Ten thousand, five thousand, three thousand, bail!"

They wake at 6 a.m. The room is filled with great beams of sunlight. One of the curtains is lying crumpled on the floor.

"Oh, God. What have you done this time?" moans Sonia, rubbing the sleep from her eyes.

At breakfast she opens up the camera app on her phone. There are three recorded moments of movement: two are for toilet visits, one for her and one for him. The third is different.

"Come and look at this." Sonia waves Simon over from the kitchen work top where he's brewing up two teas.

They both watch the ghostly grey world of the infrared recording. At 4:44 a.m. Simon slides off the bed and down onto the hardwood floor. He edges along the herringbone parquet, bringing himself to his feet next to the bi-fold doors, and takes a hold of the yellow silk curtains. Simon is wrapping himself up inside the material when the first piece of recorded audio appears.

"Bitte! Bitte!" comes his desperate call.

Now he is completely wrapped inside the curtain. Only his terrified face is poking out. Simon lets out a sickening whimper; his body collapses as he grips the curtain around him, pulling it down to the floor. He curls up in the foetal position for a few seconds then picks himself up and returns to bed, his eyes glowing ghostly white.

"What were you doing?" asks Sonia.

Simon can see she is shocked but is trying to be cool to spare his feelings. "I don't know," he says. "But I always seem to dream of saving children."

34

Publishing Splits

Sonia leaves the flat at 7 a.m. for a blood test at Dr Nal-bandian's Pregnancy Assistance Clinic. Simon retreats to the studio, opens up Logic on his laptop and double clicks on the Peski remix session. The screen comes to life as a myriad of settings; audio files and plugins collide into the electronic workstation displayed on his screen. He presses the spacebar and listens through his work. Stopping the track several times he works on minor tweaks in the mix and arrangement. After an hour of adjustment, he feels ready to bounce out a low resolution MP3 of the "Raining Down" remix. At least at this bitrate the track is un-releasable, giving him some control. He sups at a steaming cup of Douwe Egberts granulated coffee and waits for the completed version to arrive in his iTunes folder.

Hi Phillip
Please find the Peski remix attached. I will send the WAV
master files of the version and the instrumental when we can
come to agreement on the 50% of publishing. As you well
know, £200 used to be a weekly record shopping bill — a
tenth of what this kind of work used to earn. I'm not about

*to lose out on the backend payments if this remix goes on to do
well. I'm sure you understand my position as a former artist
yourself.*

    Yours Musically
    Simon

He presses return, the computer mimics the sound of an
aircraft whooshing overhead, and his phone starts ringing.

It's Sonia, sounding whispery. "I can't say much. I'm in the
toilet cubicle at work. Dr Nalbandian has got my blood work
back. My cytokines are spiking, and he says I need to have an
infusion."

"Why, what did he say?"

"He says it will lower the chance of a miscarriage."

"But we haven't even taken your eggs out yet."

"I know, but what can we do?"

"Do you believe him?"

"He has a thirty-eight percent success rate. That's the last
thing he said when I sounded stressed over the phone."

"It's your body. I'll support you."

"It's £1000 per infusion."

"I can find the extra money."

"I love you."

"I love you, too."

Simon gets out of the studio chair and moves over to his
record shelf. With a sigh he raises his right hand to touch the
spines of the vinyl in front of him. If anything represents his
passion for life, it's these outmoded objects. He starts with the
records he was sent as promo copies, picking them out from
his collection and putting them down by his feet. Record labels
used to send him promotional vinyl every day, but the brown

mailers were too big to post through the door. Simon would go to the Harlesden sorting office every week and pick up a fresh pile of the promotional vinyl that was waiting there for him: all the records looking for a little love on the dance floor. A great tide of mediocrity washed up on the shore when labels fished expensively for hits, and it was Simon's job to wade through the trash looking for treasure.

Rubbing his forehead, he tries to think of the records that mean something to him now. It's a surprise how few there are that he cares about, up there in his collection on the wall. Time has changed him. What was once sought after is now just a thought, a click away on his phone. So he's hunting down the sounds of his childhood, in search of innocence and memories of familial love. His great-grandmother comes to mind: the box-shaped woman with two fingers on one hand, who had made him watch Crown Court of a lunchtime. She lived to the age of 99, survived the invention of cars and two world wars. If he has to survive the loss of a few pieces of plastic to pay for Sonia's protection and deliver them a baby, that's nothing. Simon decides to sell them all.

By the end of the night he's listed 150 pieces of vinyl onto Discogs, the online store, raising £1000 in the process. Like the chestnut-eyed shop assistant in the Mac store reminded him, it's only other people's music after all.

The next morning Simon receives an email from Phillip:

> *Got the remix — sounding good. I'll get the accounts department to send over the £200. I'm still talking to Peski's team re: the publishing split. Can you confirm there are no samples in the production?*

Word Up
Phillip

The Basildon codpiece strikes again. Simon looks up from the Firefox browser; the face of Peter Gabriel dripping down the cover of his Melt album looks back at him, unmoved from the day he sampled a piece of piano from the shiny black vinyl. Gabriel's functioning eye pierces right into Simon's soul. He stops to wonder if Peter would mind him borrowing a piece of his music. It's only piano and bass, and Simon did chop them up to make them his own. Peter Gabriel was the first man to use a sampler on a record. He would know the score. It's just humans leaning on each other, sharing what they know.

Simon picks up the album and notices something different. The writing is green, and Simon is sure it used to be yellow before. "Games Without Frontiers" is called "*Spiel Ehne Grenze*" and "Family Snapshot" is "*SchnappschuB ein Familienfoto*". Dr Patel had warned him that if he stopped taking his tablets, his visions and misinterpretations of time could return. He leaves the studio to check the metal box on top of the fridge, the one he keeps his medications in. Last night he took his tablets. He can remember that and for the months preceding. He returns to the studio and rubs the text of the album with his thumb. It's solid green under the gloss finish.

Simon's phone starts ringing with a withheld number. He puts down the album sleeve, it falls to the floor and he answers the call.

"Simon!" comes the familiar voice.

"Yes, who is it please?"

"Tobias, and we need to talk."

Simon hangs up immediately and tries to write a text to the

weed dealer but knows he can't fall down that well again. He deletes the opening line asking for assistance and goes for a brisk walk in the dog park instead. He's meeting his mother at the airport tomorrow.

35

The Night Plane

British Airways flight 1144 banks over the silver flash of the Rhine in preparation for its descent into Dusseldorf Airport. The plane took off just before a storm moved in from the west; the fuselage bounced over the North Sea as the turmoil moved up through the Channel, pulling trees and severing electricity lines below them. The industrial heartland of the Rhine is blanketed with thick cloud from the ground all the way up to the grey belly of the ageing Boeing 737.

Descending 10,000 to 5,000 to 2,000 feet, she's nearly in. The rubber wheels thud down and the three Radcliffes hold hands through the landing. Anne has a heavy bandage around her thigh. It's holding something terrible in.

The plane is connected to the stairs of Flugsteig C. They wait for the wheelchair and head through passport control. Simon's father hands him a sealed plastic pouch. It's soft to the touch and contains an adrenalin compress. They board the sky train to Dusseldorf Central, ready to catch the slow train to Kleve for their final destination: Reichswald Forest War Cemetery.

The lights of the cities and towns dance on the river. They pass an explosion of metal pipes demarcating an ageing oil refinery. A myriad of lights and steel smokestacks gives way to swathes of empty farmland offering only endless darkness. An incomplete image of the Radcliffes reflects in the windows of the train and a stillness descends upon them. Three hours later they pull into Kleve, alight, and check in at the Rilano Hotel. The interior of the hotel is too sharp to be warm, and too clean to be comfortable. The restaurant opposite the reception serves them wild boar in cream sauce; they arrived too late to be offered a choice. The heavy food sits uncomfortably in their stomachs. They return to their rooms, where no one sleeps well.

The next morning they have breakfast, then Peter orders a taxi. A black Mercedes saloon pulls up. Simon loads the wheelchair into the taxi and Peter helps Anne in. The driver sets off for the cemetery on Grunewald Strasse. The road is flat and straight. Orange and yellow-leaved birch trees fill the gardens of the homes where Germany skirts the Dutch border, near Arnhem.

The taxi driver pulls up outside the stone entrance under a cluster of large oaks. The wind blows and an acorn drops down from a tree and bounces off the windscreen.

The white-haired driver has a gentle face and round rimmed glasses. He turns to Simon's father in the front seat and points at the graves lined up like dominoes across the majestic sea of radiant green.

"Is your family in here?" the driver says.

"Yes, my wife's father," says Peter.

"On the left or right of the cemetery?"

"I'm not sure. It's the first time we've been."

"If he is on the left, he was a murderer. Now, that will be €17, please."

"I'm sorry, on the left?" Peter says. "What do you mean?"

"They line them up in their crews of seven, how they used to fly. On the left are the bomber crews of the RAF. On the right is the army," says the driver.

A tear rolls down Anne's face as Peter hands over €30.

"Keep the change," says Peter.

"We did," says the driver through the closing door of the Mercedes. "Everything was rebuilt, and we learned. I hope you did too."

The cemetery is surrounded by ancient woodland. The entrance has two pillars with egg-shaped stone carvings on top of the sandstone blocks. Two small towers house leather books chained to the walls. The books are filled with seven thousand names.

Simon pushes Anne past the letters and through the cemetery. They meet a gardener who introduces himself as Hans.

"We're looking for the grave of Jack Robson," says Peter. "Can you help us, please?"

Hans is old, legs bowed, face worn. Simon wonders if he's here in every kind of weather, watching people cry over their family remains. Hans walks them slowly through his pristine work; each grave so neat and tidy, trying to hide the echo of the heartache underneath.

"Each of the airmen is buried with his fellow crew members," the gardener explains.

It doesn't take long for Hans to help them locate Jack and he leaves them alone. Perhaps he's seen too many of these situations to believe there's anything positive to give or say when people absorb a lifetime thrown. Anne's wheelchair is shining; the grass has washed the chrome wheels clean. She grabs Peter's hand and pulls herself out of the wheelchair.

"You taught me to walk. I'm here to say thank you," she says to the gravestone.

"Move the rose bush out the way, son, so we can see the words," says Peter.

Flying Officer J. Robson, Navigator, Royal Air Force,
20th November 1944.
Always in our thoughts, darling.
Your loving wife, Jean.

"I wish I knew what he looked like," Anne says. "There's nothing, nothing at all. Just this place here, and nobody could afford to come."

"Until now," says Peter.

"We got it done, Mum. We got it done," says Simon.

"Everyone is here apart from Bill Bellway," Peter says, moving down the row of graves. "He was missing the night they went down. Operation Hurricane on Duisberg."

"How do you know that?" asks Simon, following along, squinting into the white light of the cloudy day.

"We found your grandfather's logbooks from his time with 75 New Zealand Squadron."

"The 75 New Zealand Squadron," Simon whispers to himself, swallowing hard.

"Jack's last letter said they took a replacement wireless operator that night. Apparently changing a crew member was always seen as a bad luck sign."

"Bill Bellway. Mr Bellway from the hospital. I know that name. What did the letter say?"

"Fear, love, family, enough to break anyone down. Bill Bellway could still be alive. He might be able to help us find

174

out more about Jack, you never know." Peter rests his hands on Anne's shoulders.

"If he isn't, I know where to find his son." Simon looks at the acorns swept into a pile on the radiant green cemetery lawn.

They take a taxi back to the hotel and ready themselves for the train back to Dusseldorf to fly home.

Simon says goodbye to his parents at Heathrow and takes the express train to Paddington. He jumps onto the Circle line that takes him straight to White City. He crosses the road next to the BBC building and sprints up the path towards Queen Charlotte Hospital. Simon bursts into the andrology department and Bill Bellway Jnr is sat at his desk wearing the same burgundy-coloured clothes he last saw him in.

"Excuse me, Mr Bellway. Sorry to disturb you but I need to have a word about what our families have done."

"I'm sorry. Do you have an appointment?" Bill stands up and his chair hits against the metal of the filing cabinet.

"*Ake Ake Kia Kaha*, Mr Bellway. Just like that 75 New Zealand Squadron sticker says. I can call you Bill, can't I?" Simon knew he probably looked like a struggling mental patient from the ward next door, but he didn't care. "I've been to the graves of your dad's crew."

"My father?" Mr Bellway's old eyes shift.

"Yes, I need to know if your father is still alive, for my mother. She's dying and..."

"Your name, sir?" He looks down into his files.

"Simon, Simon Radcliffe. You know me. I came in here to give a sample just the week before, remember? You asked if I needed stimulus." Simon points to the first door where he provided his sample for the cryogenic freezer.

"You're all patients to me, Mr Radcliffe. We have to be professional. It's good that you've come back. We have a lot of legal paperwork for you to get through. I hadn't sent out your appointment letter yet."

"Paperwork? I need some answers, Bill. It's about time, don't you think?" Simon points at the squadron emblem on the iron cabinet.

Mr Bellway turns to open the draw with the sticker on it and it screeches. He pulls out an inch-thick stack of A4 papers, turns around and places them in front of Simon.

"I guess we're all just a bunch of wankers to you, eh? Your dad, please tell me, is he still alive?" Simon slaps his thighs and leans forward. Bill leans back a little and rubs at his wrinkled chin.

"Can you meet me in the café here, after work? I finish in half an hour and we can talk more easily there. I'll bring the requisite papers with me."

Simon agrees with Bill's offer, exits the andrology department and spends a little while in the charity shop. There's a jigsaw puzzle with two children in a ploughed field; above them fly two Lancaster bombers. The Steps CD has fallen backward under the aluminium walker and there's a crack in the cover. Thirty minutes pass then Simon heads over to the hospital entrance and takes a chair at a table in the centre of the café. Bill arrives and offers Simon a coffee. He walks over with their drinks, joins him at the table and places the brown folder holding Simon's papers between them.

"I've just got back from Reichswald cemetery," says Simon, pulling the folder round to his side of the table. He opens it up to reveal the papers.

"My father died ten years ago, Simon," Mr Bellway says.

"Now, if you could start with the top one, which concerns what you would like your wife to do with your sperm if you were to pass away."

Simon rolls the pen between his fingers. "These are not the easiest scenarios to imagine. First, you tell me: before he died, did your dad ever tell you about what they did, during the war?"

"Can you just concentrate on the paperwork for now, please? I can tell you more in a moment, but these are life or death decisions for your family."

"I want to know about *your* family, Bill, because mine is falling apart."

"If you don't sign off on these consent papers, Simon, we may as well go and put your sample in the bin right away."

"We could have been family, joined by grief, you know?" Simon signs the first paper consenting to Sonia's right to make a baby with his sperm if he dies.

"I knew my father flew," says Mr Bellway. "He never talked about it, except maybe once around Christmas when he drank too much. Stood outside in the garden and cried in the snow."

"Did he run away the night they went down, or did he just get lucky, Bill?"

"My father didn't run away. He had a sore throat that night."

"What? Is that all he had? Really?" Simon pushes the papers away from him.

"He survived because he had a bad case of laryngitis. They wouldn't let him fly, or so my mother told me."

"The night they went to Duisburg?" Simon pulls the papers back toward him.

"I really don't know but some things that hurt get buried

away." Bill lowers his voice. "Like everyone, you do what you have to do to live and get on. Holding on will kill you just as much as letting go."

Simon is distracted because Mr Bellway keeps glancing over his shoulder, toward the café door. Looking over, Simon sees Dr Frau Brandt watching them through the windows. He feels the walls closing in. He doesn't know if they're here to help him or destroy him.

"I came here in case you had any photographs of the crew to give to my mother," says Simon. "She was only three years old when they went down. She doesn't even know what he looked like. I'm sure you can see, I just want to complete the circle before, well, before it's too late." Simon pins his rising emotion back down into the centre of his chest.

"My father wouldn't talk about it." Mr Bellway's eyes glaze over as he lowers his voice. "Never said a thing about the night he escaped the fate of your grandfather."

"So, you *do* know about that night?" Simon puts his weak hand down on the papers in front of him.

"We had another family approach us, from the same squadron. It was about twenty years ago now. My dad claimed he didn't know any of them."

Simon sits back in his chair as he turns his palms up to face the ceiling. "But he's in the logbooks for sixteen operations with that crew. My dad has the paperwork. Your father's name is in there, plain as day."

"I guess he blanked it out. Wouldn't you want to forget killing women and babies every night..." Mr Bellway's voice tails off as he looks over to the lift. Simon follows his eyes, the lift door is closing, a golden stethoscope glints in the light before they shut.

178

"Forgetting your friends isn't really how this should go though, Bill. You know they had no choice once they were in. Men doing frightening things to the best of their ability, doing what they were told had to be done."

"I know, Simon. I know."

"What about Dr Frau Brandt — why was she watching us just now? Tobias? Dr Untermeyer? What do they want from me?"

"There is so much I could tell you, Simon. But in matters of life and death we have to remain as professional as we can."

36

French Number 1

Simon is back in the studio. Tiny pieces of fake leather are falling onto the Turkish rug as he shifts his weight from side to side on the office chair. Pricing up his record collection on Discogs is taking him longer than he thought. Dr Nalbandian has got both Simon and Sonia on edge. It seems there's always a new problem with the IVF treatment. If it's not Sonia's blood, it's Simon's diet. And he's been too scared to tell the doctor that he hasn't produced a sperm sample since the prostate operation left him tender, confused and emotionally sore. Is he going to become a father when he can no longer function as a man? He is too scared to find out. There are many things they don't tell you about getting old.

Phillip Storey's number comes up on Simon's phone. He picks it from under the black record deck and disconnects the charging cable.

"Phillip, glad you've called."

"It's a hit, Simon!" Phillip's voice sounds like he's been huffing helium.

"What is?"

"Your remix version. We promoted it digitally in France and it's already been playlisted on Radio Nova, NRJ and

Mouv!" Phillip squeals.

"What the hell are you talking about?" Simon shouts in desperation. "I only sent you a low-resolution MP3, and we didn't resolve the main issue with the publishing splits."

"Chill out, Simon. This track is really going to go. You *are* sure there are no samples in it, aren't you?" Phillip says, lowering his voice back to a normal pitch.

"What if there were?" Simon stops the excitement dead.

"You can't tell me that now," Phillip replies in shock.

"If you've released a low quality MP3 of my remix and didn't even bother to let me know, you're at best stupid and at worst, well, who knows?"

"I'm sorry, Simon. I can have a word with the accounts department, send you a few grand." Phillip's voice shifts, rising into a pathetic whisper. "Call it quits, still be friends?"
Simon lets a long pause linger. He looks into Peter Gabriel's one good eye on the cover of the Melt album.

"How much are we talking?"

"Would 5K sort you out?" punts Phillip with a whine in his voice.

"Give me 10K and I'm out of the picture. For good."

"That's a lot of money."

"How much are you earning off the PRS on the French playlists?" Simon rams the play arm into his spokes.

"OK, 10K." Phillip sighs. "I'll see what I can do."

"Get the money to me before the end of the week, Phillip."

37

Interruption Inflagrante

Sonia is stood in front of the slate grey metallic Bosch fridge. As she studies its contents, Simon sees her face lit up by the low glow of the twenty-five watt light. The Gonal-F synthetic hormone bottles stored next to the eggs are dwindling, the IVF cycle is counting down. Soon Dr Nalbandian's surgeons will be going inside her fallopian tubes and reaching for her eggs. Simon is sat in his chair in front of the television. Although Sonia is proficient at self-injecting, he offers his help all the same.

"I'm fine," Sonia replies, moving over to rest her hand on his left shoulder. "But we need to run a test, don't we?"

"A test on what?" says Simon, looking her in the eyes.

"On you," she says with a smile.

Simon furrows his brow. "On me? Not again."

"You know what I mean." Sonia points at Simon's crotch.

"Oh," says Simon, dejected.

"If you can't make a sample when we need it, then we have to ask ourselves, what has this all been for?" Sonia says.

"I know." Simon shifts uncomfortably in his chair. "But it just feels all wrong, down there."

"How?" she asks, rubbing his shoulder.

"To put it simply, it feels burned to a crisp."

"Oh, Simon. I'm sorry I didn't know it was that bad. But we can't rely on the frozen samples so we really need to know if... if we can keep it all natural, in the moment and go with the flow."

"I had to sign a lot of papers in the café at the hospital," says Simon. "Mr Bellway's dad flew with my grandfather. He's a bit embarrassed about it because *his* grandfather survived by getting ill. How weird is that?"

"You're obsessed," says Sonia. "I've told you we have to focus now if we're going to have a chance of getting pregnant."

"You'll be pleased to know I gave you written permission to start an army if I happen to die."

"That's so romantic." Sonia squeezes his shoulder gently. "Now, can you still make him stand up and look happy?"

"I don't know. It's just the memory of the biopsy rods and the catheter."

Sonia puts her hands up to her ears. "OK, OK. Stop. That's enough."

"But you're right. We really must try." Simon sits forward in the chair.

"Shall I go and put something on?" says Sonia.

"Get the injections done, then come down and we'll give it a try."

Downstairs, Simon has pulled his pants down and is sat back in his chair. Sonia arrives and within thirty seconds it becomes apparent he is capable of standing to attention.

"Does it make you happy?" Sonia asks with her hips thrust to the side and a glint in her eye.

Simon nods slowly and reaches for the warm welcoming skin, his sensory imagination up and running.

"Looks like Dr Untermeyer didn't break it then."

Their giggling is interrupted when Simon's phone rings on the coffee table next to him. It's his father. He lets it ring out, too absorbed in this ancient preoccupation. A text pings after the missed call. Simon looks away from Sonia's breasts to read it from the corner of his eye: *Simon, you have to come home, as soon as you can.*

38

The RVI

Simon has been driving for three hours; the trains to Newcastle were cancelled this morning. He's hired a Ford Focus from Green Motion on Edgeware Road and it's taken him an hour to get out of North West London. His mum and dad aren't answering their phones and his perceptions have taken on a different slant — a sense of emotional nausea is unfolding in slow motion. The M1 takes him past Nottingham, then Sheffield, the visual reminders of the stages of many journeys home. North Yorkshire starts with its wild lands, the dank green earth and funny place names: Leeming Bar, Catterick, Darlington, Sedgefield, Coxhoe and Bowburn. Crossing the River Tyne over Blaydon Bridge, its rotund concrete struts are like grey shins stuffed deep into the riverbed. The tide is out, and the mud flats shine like fireglazed stone. Simon exits for the airport, Junction 7 up the A69. A commercial jet is making its approach through a distant cloud as he heads for the final straight into the village of Dinningland.

Simon pulls the car up on the block paving driveway. At the door, he takes in a deep breath and rings the bell. There's no reply. He exhales and walks round the back of the house. By the kitchen door, Anne's empty wheelchair has been left at an untidy angle in the driveway and there's no sign of the Ford Orion. Above the thicket hedge surrounding the well-kept quarter acre, the sky is shaded powder blue. Soon it will darken, a deep black blue with a tiny glimmer — an endless dusk that refuses the sun a rest.

Simon calls his father again. Peter answers for the first time in twenty-four hours, his hello followed by the beep of a heart monitor.

"Come into town, son. We're in the A&E of the RVI," Peter tells him in a voice that seems far too ordinary for what is happening.

"I'll be there as soon as I can," Simon replies.

He presses the phone's red button to end the call, his consciousness shifting outside of himself into hyper reality.

The autopilot inside drives him down the spine road and into town. He parks up between the rows of white lines in the empty Royal Victoria Infirmary car park. It's 11 p.m. on a summer evening, things are quiet and speeding on.

Inside the ward, Anne is laid up high in a wheeled bed. Electronic equipment surrounds her, breathing out, breathing in.

"I'm really sick, son," she says, turning her distressed head to tell him. The words, no more than a whisper, drown in the whir of medical equipment and aircon.

Simon swallows hard. "Yes, Mum."

Hours go unnoticed, time disappears, melting away in the fug of chemically released emotions. Eventually Simon and Peter realize they will have to go home, this initial separation a trial period for the new normal hurtling toward them into the unknown.

The next day Simon returns without Peter. Anne has been

moved to the lung ward of the Freeman Hospital. Pneumonia is just a symptom of what's really going on.

In the bed to Anne's right, a paper-skinned woman sits up, her tiny body supporting a head with a face pitted like a bleached pear and riven by chain smoking.

Simon sees five young, male trainee doctors following a petite female specialist like gangly ducklings. He realizes they're coming to his mother's bed to deliver the news.

The tallest trainee pulls the green curtain around Anne's bed. He looks nervous, tucking his blonde curly hair behind his ears. He smiles at Anne as the rest look on like scared children in an aquarium.

"You need to have a lot of parties, and soon," the specialist explains after a long list of places the "C" word has travelled inside of Anne's body.

The trainee doctors look on studiously, but their fidgeting hands give everything away. Simon imagines that the specialist called all her trainees one by one and said: "Come, quickly now. I'll show you how this is done: the code of practice for telling a patient about the big one."

Here it comes for Simon, like a silent freight train, steaming through his body, crushing, crushing, crushing on. He tries to look his mother in the eye without imploding. Even the pale-faced lady in the next bed gasped when she overheard the news through the flimsy green curtain.

It is the only time that Simon has seen his mother cry in forty years of ill health. For twenty-five seconds the concept sits there as she absorbs her projected demise. Then she stops crying, dries her eyes and thanks the specialist for doing the hard job, taking the time to tell her it is nearly over, done.

Through a gap in the curtain, Simon sees a nurse

approaching the death party. The nurse pulls the curtain back and suddenly all the doctors have disappeared. The air is still, lips are pursed, then the moment is gone — just the time moving on.

Simon leaves his mother to the gentle small talk that springs from the incalculable well of Northern humanity. He drives back from the hospital to break the news to his father.

"The doctor said we have to have a lot of parties, and soon," Simon explains in the car on the way back to the hospital.

On the radio, Billy Joel is telling them that working too hard can give you a heart attack. "Movin' Out" is playing through the car's cheap speakers on Radio 2. The song reminds Simon of how it had all begun. The family had been to the Lido De Jesolo, near Venice, in '76, and everyone's skin had been hurting from the sun. Cancer at the bottom of Anne's calf was where things had started to go wrong. Now, Simon tells his father, it's in her adrenal glands, her bones, lymph nodes and the lining of her lungs.

"Apply the adrenalin pouch firmly," was all that Simon heard from the doctor who called by to see how Anne's life was passing.

A brandy hangover is blurring the quantity of information flashing through the centre of his soul.

Simon makes a mental note to finish that playlist he promised his mother. It will be the only time she will be taken somewhere ever again: figuratively, of course, because soon she'll be in a purple palliative care bed, wheeled into the family lounge and placed horizontally into her favourite place by the window. The place she sat before the metastasis burrowed home.

The next day a taxi door slams shut outside the lounge

window. Sonia has arrived. She's still in her work clothes — black pants, blazer and shirt — ready to dress the house for the party. Anne is sat up on the purple bed with her back supported by cushions. She's acting as though it's an average Sunday afternoon. Peter's lost look suggests he can't tell if it's the Oramorph painting opiate edges around the norm, or his own reality dissolving in front of him.

Sonia and Simon jump in the Ford Focus and head for the garden centre on the outskirts of Dillington. They return with plants that bloom in lilac and position them on the windowsills around the plastic purple death bed. A banner made of letters connected by string and printed on silver squares is placed across the chimney breast. It reads *Welcome Home*. The gas fire below it lies dormant. It's twenty-eight degrees outside. The windows are open and warm air is moving in.

Sonia sits down next to Anne and holds her hand.

"Now, did they sort out your blood, Sonia?" asks Anne, life beaming strong from her focused eyes.

"Yes, Anne. At first I didn't want to do it, but I listened to the encouragement you gave me. I think it's going to work this time," Sonia says, stroking her arm.

Simon notices the sapphire in Anne's birthstone ring almost matches the colour of the veins in her hand.

Dr Nalbandian's Pregnancy Assistance Clinic have been on the phone. The day is getting nearer. Hormone injections are pushing Sonia to the apex of the baby-making zone. Sonia will have to go back home to London tomorrow.

The plastic-fitted windows are wound open in the lounge.

"I'll be thinking of you," is the last thing Anne says to Sonia before the taxi arrives.

Simon watches Sonia climb into the taxi as she wipes a tear from her eye. Outside the balmy azure of summer welcomes the world as forgiving. A small butterfly keeps dancing round the patterns on the curtains. It flies further into the room and rests on Anne's hair for a while. Peter walks into the room and Simon shushes him as the butterfly takes off to find the open window.

39

Last Requests

Simon is taking in the family garden. Music seeps from the lounge windows as the welcome home party continues. The plant world explodes with life, like the cells forming unwanted growths inside of Anne. Simon is getting through it by adding songs to the Spotify playlist on his phone; he's not sure if he will be listening to any music at the after party. They're not quite there after all.

He returns to the lounge and sits next to his mother. Billy Joel's "Only The Good Die Young" is getting a big response. Now "Always A Woman To Me" is getting to everyone. The song ends and for the first time in a day Anne comes to life and opens her eyes fully for the last time. She looks directly at Simon.

"We'll Gather Lilacs In The Spring Again," she requests.

"It was your grandmother Jean's favourite song," says Peter. "She always thought Jack would come back one day."

"Yes, I will find it on my phone," says Simon. "Mum, I got told by a doctor in London to ask you about Homberg. What is it that happened there?"

"Brother Alan will know," says Anne.

Simon finds the Anne Zeigler and Webster Booth version

and presses play. The pretty string motif lights up the room and the curtains blow a little on the summer breeze. Webster Booth opens up the solo chorus as Anne drifts off.

When Anne wakes from her drug-induced haze, she asks for her daddy. "When is he going to come home?" she says, her eyes innocent.

"Alan, your brother, is coming now," says Peter. "He remembers, darling."

Peter goes to the door to let Alan in. He arrives in his best suit clutching some lilac flowers.

Simon goes to make them all tea in the kitchen. He takes the biggest cup over to Alan. "We went to your dad's grave for the first time."

"That's a lovely thing to do," says Alan. "I've always wanted to go."

"What happened in Homberg, Alan?" Simon asks.

"I've got all the letters, but I can't bring myself to read them," Alan says. "I was only eight years old. Some things you spend a lifetime forgetting." Alan looks like a lost boy who had chosen not to cry for sixty years.

Simon notices his father's face is also childlike, ashen, reverting back to where they came from.

The Macmillan nurse keeps injecting Anne with morphine now. One doctor said her back was about to snap, said he could operate and put a pin in if they wanted. Simon told the doctor to forget it and chased the Happy Service for a plastic support so Anne could sit up — watch Netflix with ease at home. Another doctor talked of a new drug that would stimulate the immune system.

"Do you know how many places the cancer is?" Simon asks all the different doctors in frustration.

"I see what you mean," they reply, after consulting Anne's growing notes.

Simon can barely conceal the resentment. "It's too late," he says. "You should have found it earlier."

"There really is nothing that can be done once it spreads like this," another doctor explains in a manner that Simon held tight.

Don't be angry. It won't change anything, Simon keeps telling himself over and over again.

One of Anne's eyes is half closed now, as if she is winking to let them know what's to come. The dentist came yesterday, put some veneers back on, now that time has passed and gone. Cousins came from Canada at the drop of a hat and hoped that they were heard: took some time with Anne alone.

"Under the stairs," are the last words Anne says to Simon.

"Yes, of course, Mum," he replies, not able to process what it means.

"Don't be scared of the shutdown," Sonia said to Simon last night on the phone. "That's the stage when all the listening is done."

"Sonia is pregnant!" Simon shouts out in the family lounge.

"She is! She's pregnant... Mum!" The words crushed at the back of his throat with a rising note as he squeezes her hand. Anne squeezes back with a tight short action. Simon wanted the words to be the last she heard, no matter what the outcome. What's a white lie between a dying mother and her son?

Both of her eyes are closed now. Peter, his sister Kate, and Simon hold Anne's hands in unison — a human circuit with one essential component blown.

"Thank you," Simon whispers into the still white light,

now the disconnected whirr of the death rattle has begun.

An hour passes in silence and the birds sing because they don't know what's going on.

"I'll bring those letters when I next see you, Simon. I have to go now, get back home," says Alan as he slips out the front door.

"When they shut down, do they ever come back?" Simon turns to ask the MacMillan nurse, her blue eyes piercing into him.

"One woman in Wallsend did," the nurse replies, strong hands placed firmly on hips, arms strengthened from lifting helpless people up and waiting for their ends to come.

"What did she say when she came back around?" Simon asks in a whisper.

"That all she heard was everyone saying she was dead," she answers, walking across the room in her purple uniform, which matches the waterproof mattress of the palliative care bed. She kneels on the pastel pinks of the rug and opens her black medicine bag to find her largest morphine injection.

"That's a lot to take in," Simon stumbles over the images colliding into him.

"It didn't last."

"How long?" Simon asks with his hands pressed against his cheeks, like Edvard Munch's scream.

"She died the next day," Mary concludes with a soft shrug.

"Do you want a cup of coffee?" is all that Simon can say — a chance to move and escape the walls closing in.

"Yes, two brown sugars, please," Mary replies, preparing the last morphine injection in the summer light of the lounge window.

Mary waits until Simon is gone. He watches her through a

crack in the door as the nurse returns to the purple care bed, lifts up Anne's nightshirt and pushes the coup de grace in.

Somehow everyone manages some form of sleep that night. Peter is in a sleeping bag on the floor below Anne's bed. The rattle is fading. The bomb falling toward them all in slow motion, hour by hour, ready to break them up into a million pieces.

Simon's phone rings.

A chest that was rattling its last breaths, is faltering, then finally still.

"She has gone, gone today," Simon mumbles into his phone.

"I'm sorry..." Sonia sounds lost in the distance between them.

"It got so bad, it had to come," Simon says.

"I don't know what to say," says Sonia. "I loved her a lot too."

Sonia's voice crackles and drops out as Simon walks up the garden past the Nikko Blue hydrangea. He holds one of the plant's heart-shaped leaves between the fingers of his left hand.

"She always said that the best way to go would be a party, then you take a tablet and you're gone," says Simon, unaware that he is digging his thumb into a vein on the leaf, and the sticky green chlorophyll is leaking out and staining his skin. Two powder lilac cupido minimus butterflies dance around the hydrangea's blooms.

"I'm sorry, Simon," says Sonia, and Simon can tell she's measuring her words. "But if we want to have the baby, you have to come home to London now."

"Now? But mum's still here, in the lounge." Simon stares at

the green stain on his finger with his head bowed. Around him the birds are singing, and the summer is in full swing.

"It's the last egg we have, remember," Sonia says, sounding desperate.

"Our only chance?" Simon has lost track of everything. A few seconds of silence holds in the hot air.

"She would want you to come back too." Sonia delivers pragmatism just like Anne.

"She squeezed my hand when I lied about us being pregnant. She must have heard me, like you said," Simon's voice quivers a little as he explains the final moment between them.

"Hopefully it won't be a lie," Sonia says with optimistic steel.

"Telling people what they want to hear is not always a lie, I guess." Simon steadies himself, leaning his shoulder against the wall at the back of the bungalow. "The last thing she said was 'Under the stairs', the Oramorph doing its thing."

Three hundred miles away from each other they pause and breathe.

"I can be there in about six hours," Simon estimates, taking into account the abundance of 50 mph zones littering the M1.

"That's within the time window, but just get here as fast as possible. Today is our only day. It's a lot, I know."

Simon looks at his mother in the family home for one last time. Peter is in the bed with her. Simon takes a pair of scissors from the kitchen draw, walks in silence to the side of the bed and cuts a piece of hair from his mother's head, where the butterfly had landed, caught for a moment in the light beaming from the sun. He touches Peter's shoulder to wake him.

"I have to go back to London, Dad, for the baby. I'll be back as soon as I can."

It's all Simon can manage. He turns from the sight of his father's rib cage shaking and places his left hand on the brass handle of the lounge door. With a twist he leaves the moment that will last forever in the room.

Inside the Ford Focus, it's roasting. The car has been out all morning in the sun. The drive back to London is serene as if nothing has really happened. Autopilot on, stomach churning, Simon wonders if he will be able to produce a sample good enough to make a baby from.

Eventually he arrives at Staples Corner, where the M1 meets the Roman Edgeware Road. Two miles down, past the electronics shops, the Hilton Hotel where he hired the car appears behind the Westway flyover. Simon exits the Edgeware Road and drives the hire car deep into the hotel's bowels. Round the tight carpark corners he turns, corkscrewing himself down, deeper into the earth. Parking up between the concrete pillars, he gets out of the Ford Focus with a slam of the door. He heads for the exit, climbs the airless staircase that leads to the foyer of the Hilton, and returns the car keys in the hire company overnight box.

Outside the hotel, Simon grimaces in the daylight, takes in the polluted air and sets off walking toward Harley Street. He is ready to grasp at their genetic future, ready to try and fill the gaps left by the limitless love they lost in the north, back up there, back home.

40

In the Basement

Behind the enamel blue door of the London Child Factory, agitated couples queue on the stairs leading to Dr Nalbandian's office. Some of the men in the queue have found themselves making love against their own wishes. "For the cause", their wives remind them, like the IRA collecting money in the pubs of Kilburn.

The banker who berated Simon in the Ilithios Members Club is blocking the halfway point of the stairs. His powder blue eyes agitate around the shapes in the raised pattern of the 1930s wallpaper lining the stair wall. Shuffling his feet from side to side with frustration, his two grand shoes shine proud like polished mahogany.

Simon calls Sonia from the hallway but there is no reply. He takes a seat in the waiting room and a text vibrates his phone.

Down in the basement, it reads.

He heads down the stone stairs into the dark, his clothes brushing against the cold tight passageway. In a poorly lit nook, a private nurse stands with her back to him. She's reading through blood results.

"I'm looking for Sonia," says Simon, and the nurse jumps.

"Sorry, Sonia?" comes the reply.

"My wife." Simon's voice is trapped in the tight Georgian tunnel, plastered and painted to feel like now.

"This room has many Sonias," says the nurse with a sigh.

"Radcliffe, Sonia Radcliffe," says Simon, over-pronouncing the syllables.

The nurse turns to a black metal filing cabinet in the cramped corridor and pulls a handle. The draw opens with a low groan and she fingers through a thick clump of papers hung vertically in the draws.

"Ah, yes. Sonia has just been extracted. You're just in time for the window," says the nurse with a bright rising tone.

"The window?" Simon says, leaning against the tunnel wall.

"The impregnation window," the nurse replies, pushing her tortoise shell glasses back up her nose and cocking her head back. "You can go back to the entrance and up the stairs to the second floor. There's a bathroom past Dr Nalbandian's office."

The nurse hands Simon the sperm collection jar. He runs his finger along the indentations of the white lid and stares at the blank adhesive paper label.

"Can I see my wife before I go up?" he asks, stopping himself from telling the nurse about his mother.

"She's in room D. It's the fifth one on your right." The nurse points down a side corridor past an old photocopying machine lying dormant.

"Shouldn't this have my name on it, or Sonia's even?" Simon twists the sample jar round in the yellow of the strip light.

"I'll do the paperwork once you've completed the delivery of the sample. Leave it with the nurse at reception on the ground floor," the nurse tells him.

Simon moves on to find Sonia laid out on a small bed in the

egg extraction room. He takes her hand and squeezes it gently. Just like his mother twenty-four hours ago, she squeezes back. Life is still out there, fighting.

"I'm off to the bathroom to give my sample. I made it in time," Simon proclaims proudly, his voice wavering.

Sonia smiles and tears stream down her face. Simon stops one with his thumb, sits on the edge of the bed and kisses her cheek before heading upstairs.

Simon hides the collection jar with the tight grip of his fist, climbs past the queue on the stairs and enters a tiny 1950s-style chrome finished bathroom. He stares himself down in the mirror and the imaginary Queen bassline kicks in: he's definitely under pressure. With military precision, it's all over in seconds. The sample arrives black as the night, stained with the memory of his prostate operation.

Simon falls forward and holds himself still with his weak wrist against the mirror. This is all his body has got to give. He steadies himself and thrusts the burned memories of the past down into his pocket. Clutching at his last chance of a family, he passes the banker on the stairs and wishes him luck. He hands the dark sample over to the nurse at reception.

"My mother died today," he says, his emotion exploding to the surface, gasping out for oxygen. "Please make sure it works this time. We can't take it anymore."

On the tube Sonia clings to Simon and they sway as one by the exit doors. At home they occupy time by doing nothing. Grief swirls like a phantom breathing their air.

The Assisted Pregnancy Clinic rings Sonia five days later. It seems Dr Nalbandian must have found something living in the murky sample. One of the eggs has made it through the zygote stage and has become a blastocyst. The egg is rated with a grade B. Dr Nalbandian puts it back into Sonia on a Wednesday afternoon. That night she lies out horizontally on the sofa at home. Simon joins her. They make a pact not to cry, and they pray for the blastocyst to embed in the wall of her womb.

The next day Simon takes a call from the urology department of Charing Cross Hospital; he has to go to his local GP to test the level of prostate specific antigen in his blood. He calls the GP and they ask him to come in as soon as he can. Sonia is packing their suitcase at the foot of the bed. Tomorrow is Simon's mother's funeral and they're headed back up to Newcastle. Simon has already dug out his dress shoes, the ones that danced at weddings not so long ago; now they gather dust for a different kind of function.

"I'm just heading out to catch up with someone," Simon says.

Sonia looks up from the pile of neatly folded clothing, caught off guard and a little stressed. "OK. But don't be too long, yeah? We have to be at Kings Cross just after 1."

Simon crosses the road outside the church and heads to the GP's for his follow up PSA test. He catches sight of Allyssa out of the corner of his eye. She's waiting outside the church with a transparent bag containing a record with what looks like Peter Gabriel's face on the sleeve. Simon takes cover behind the bus stop and watches her, wondering why his hypnotherapist is so close to home. As Allyssa enters the church, the record bag swings, revealing the text on the cover. It's green and identical to the one he just sold. Simon takes a seat at the bus stop and starts to sweat. He opens up the Discogs app on his phone. The address he sent the album to is in Hampstead, under the name J. Volkmar. The hiss of the doors of an arriving bus break his concentration. He's late for his appointment.

Simon signs in at the GP's and is called for his blood sample. He asks to lie on the bed and thinks about why Alyssa would have the record. Does she live in Hampstead with J? Who is J? Simon avoids fainting in the doctor's surgery and returns home. He eats a ham and mustard sandwich Sonia has made for him. They eat their lunch together, sitting in the bay window overlooking the street.

"My hypnotherapist is down the street in the church, and I think she might be the one who bought my Peter Gabriel album. There was a scratch on the first track that made the record jump. It would get stuck in time. I disclosed it on the description. The buyer overpaid a lot for it, though. I thought my Paypal had tripped out. Was Allyssa with Johan at the Four Core party?"

"This is not helping, Simon," Sonia says gently. "Please, don't go there again."

The couple retreat inside their heads. They exit the flat in a hurry. Nothing is said as the sound of their suitcase wheels echo round an empty Queens Park. They take the tube to Kings Cross, find platform 0 and head for the quiet coach of the 1 o'clock train to Newcastle.

The train pulls in four hours later with a warm breeze brushing through the five bridges lining the Tyne. Everything is the same, except no one is there to meet them. They take a taxi to Dillingland in silence as they close in on the family bungalow.

Anne's sister Pat answers the door to let them in. She purses her lips and points to the bedroom where Simon finds Peter weeping at the base of the marital bed.

Simon leaves his father and sits in the chair he always used to sit in, right up close to the television — all those times when he first came back from college and talked for hours and hours to his mum. He flicks through the channels and watches a Top of the Pops re-run. It's 1983, the sound of a dreamy synth pad promises distant closeness as Limahl prances across the screen in loose fitting dayglo. Kajagoogoo's "Too Shy" flicks a switch in his memory banks: Simon is in his school uniform pulling tricks in his mother's wheelchair on the smooth tarmac outside the window. Now, he sees the chair folded up and the wheels are rested against the vegetable rack screwed to the kitchen wall. Someone should really call the Happy Service to come and pick up the wheelchair, but nobody wants to let anything go.

Simon makes them dinner and Peter excuses himself to mourn at full volume in the bedroom again. After giving his father a few minutes, Simon goes to check on him. He has noticed his father's pain comes in grief tsunamis that last for fifteen minutes until his body can't take him through the grinder anymore. Peter looks up from his prone position down on the floor. Simon realizes his father is now exactly five years old. He hasn't lost his wife; he's lost his replacement mother too. He's just too young to understand it all.

A warm breeze envelopes them as they climb into Peter's Orion and travel to the West Road Crematorium. The radio is playing Supertramp's "The Logical Song". Life used to be so wonderful. Turning acceptance into the acceptable is what will lay ahead for them now.

The men carry the coffin into the crematorium, where Sade's "Your Love Is King" is on loop. The 1980s were good to this family, when they were all growing older, and so good at being young. The service is packed to the rafters and everyone has a touch of lilac somewhere in their suit. Simon took control of communications for the funeral and could feel his mother say to him, "Please, not in black, son."

Behind the velvet curtain they are going to send Anne back into space, make her small again, back to where it all began.

Anne's brother Alan is at the end of the pew holding a small box filled with letters from their father — the letters Alan has never been able to read. He was eight years old when it happened, he'd once told Simon. Everyone in the house had been screaming, "Not him, not Jack. Not Jack!"

Now, Alan hands the wooden box to Simon over the worn crematorium pew. "Your mother would have wanted you to have them," is all he can whisper.

The top of the box looks like a blurred Renaissance artwork. A hundred fading letters are folded up inside. Part of Alan died when the letters stopped and the man who wrote them came down from the sky.

41

Cytokines & Sample Mines

Back home in London Simon is putting his dress shoes away when his phone rings. It's the Charing Cross urology department.

"I have some news, Mr Radcliffe," says a friendly male voice in a Scottish accent. "It's your PSA."

Simon sits down to ready himself "You may as well put me out of my misery," he says.

"Your PSA is very low, Mr Radcliffe. In fact, it's down to 0.3 now."

"Is that a good or bad thing?"

"It means your surgery was a success and your cancer has gone."

Relief floods over Simon and he shivers with the thought of the day the doctors got so deep inside of him. He puts his hand over the receiver for a minute to gather his thoughts. "I appreciate all you've done for me," he says. "What was the name of the surgeon, please. So I can send a card or something over?"

"Dr Untermeyer was your surgeon on the day."

Simon sits on the bed for a moment, takes in a big breath and calls Sonia. She's at work in the office of Skrape. He tells her the news.

"Yes! That's incredible news, honey. I've had a call from Dr Nalbandian this morning, as well. We have to take the pregnancy test later today," she half whispers to hide the spectre of maternity leave from her boss.

"Shall we do it together again tonight? Or do you think that will jinx it like before?"

"Don't be silly. I'll pick a test up at the chemist's on my way."

"Is it too much to ask for two positives after yesterday?"

"He said my blood results are still full of cytokines, and it's likely to stay that way." Sonia sounds resolute.

"What does that mean?"

"It means, if I am pregnant, we'll have to keep paying for infusions throughout the full term."

"How much? Did he say?"

"Anything up to 10K." Her words hang in the air

Simon fills the space. "We've been trapped by wanting it too much. Stuck in a damned loop, frozen in time."

"You can't look at it like that. We just have to keep going." The line crackles as Sonia's voice drops out for a second. "Your mum will be watching over us, OK?"

"Hang on a minute, I've got another call."

Simon says goodbye to Sonia and takes the call from Phillip Storey.

"Hi, Simon. I'm sorry I've been quiet. It's this remix."

"The Peski one? Alright, fire away."

"You won't believe what's happened in the last few days," Phillip says.

"Try me."

"Peter Gabriel's management are suing us. They claimed the remix had a sample of "Family Snapshot", in your version, Simon."

"I see."

"Well it doesn't, does it?" says Phillip anxiously.

"It might have the odd bit chopped up in there. You never came back with a contract, so do you expect me to really care?" Simon falls back into his chair.

"They're positioning to claim ownership of the whole song, Simon." Phillip sounds scared, on the verge of business tears.

"So, recall my remix from the stations that are playing it, and use the label's original version then," says Simon.

"But the remix is the hit version and it's out there now," Phillip shouts. "Nothing can change that. It's a digital file. The past is now impossible to throw away."

"Life's not meant to be easy," Simon spits back. "If you recall, you gave me £200 for three day's work, then decided to release it without my permission. I would have disclosed the sample in the contract so that's a problem of your own making."

"Peski is suicidal," Phillip whimpers.

"I'm sorry to hear that, Phillip. Speak to Peter Gabriel. He was the first artist to use a sampler and he's a good guy, I hear."

"Really?" Phillip perks up.

"It was a Fairlight CMI Series II."

"I don't care about the bloody equipment, Simon. Do you mean he might be open to letting us off then?"

"That's your problem. After Gabriel's publishing, you'll have to clear it with the label as well, and if you don't respect the process, why should anyone care?"

Simon presses the red disconnect button on his phone as Phillip carries on pleading at the end of the line.

Outside in the downstairs garden, a dirty flood of grey water is escaping from the drain. Used lumps of toilet paper are flowing out into the street like a rotten flotilla. A Thames Water van arrives and drives through the mess. Three workers wearing hi-vis jackets exit the van and carry a hose reel onto the property. The Thames Water engineers put the red metal reel down next to the recycling bins. Simon watches on as they set about lifting the drain cover with two iron hooks. They pull some black cable off the reel and check the camera on its tip with a rub of the finger. The tip is fed like a worm down into the sewers.

Simon tries to make out the image on the small screen in the downstairs front garden, but the engineers are stood in the way. He opens the sash window to ask them. The engineers turn round and look up.

"What's the problem, gentlemen?" says Simon.

"It's a big piece of material. It looks like silk," says the bespectacled head engineer in his orange jacket, with his black hair slicked back.

"How did that get down there?" Simon leans out the window for a better look.

"We don't know. It's normally baby wipes that block up the pipes."

"There's no babies in here," says Simon. "Thanks for sorting it out all the same."

He closes the window and the lead weights in the sash boxes bang against the Edwardian wood frame. The kettle in the kitchen comes to a boil. Simon makes himself a cup of tea and the doorbell rings. He places the steaming cup on the table in the bay window and heads downstairs, expecting a water engineer. The lock clicks as he twists it clockwise and the door opens to a flood of stale London air.

"Hello, Mr Radcliffe," says Bill Bellway Jnr. He is stood

at the door, looking as old and frail as Simon's own father. In his hand is a thin A4 envelope, which he is tapping against the side of his leg. "I'm sorry, this isn't very professional. I just couldn't leave things this way."

"It's alright, Bill. I can call you, Bill, can't I? We can forget about the paperwork. I don't need the frozen samples. I don't have cancer anymore and everything still works down there." Simon points down toward his zip.

"I have something for you." Mr Bellway hands over the envelope. "It arrived by post from New Zealand this morning."

"Timing is everything," muses Simon, taking the envelope from him.

Mr Bellway turns to walk away. "I'm on my lunch break. I have to get back to the andrology department, Mr. Radcliffe."

"I understand, Bill. It's a tough job. All those people playing with themselves in shot of your ear. Careful you don't trip on the silk down there."

"Remember: it was laryngitis, more than just a sore throat," shouts Bill as he retreats cautiously down the path, past the leaking drains. With a slow wave, he heads back down the street.

Simon climbs back up the stairs and heads over to his tea on the table. He sits down, takes a sip and opens the flap of the envelope. Inside is a single large black and white photograph. Its edges are irregular, and parts of the picture have faded away. Seven men in dark Royal Air Force uniform are stood in front of a fuselage marked NN710 AA-Q (Queenie). It's a copy of the service picture, the one which Grandma Jean had lost. The only photo ever taken of Grandfather Jack. He's stood next to radio operator Bill Bellway Snr, their smiles unconvincing, brushed over with fear.

Simon takes the paper packet out of his pocket, containing a piece of his mother's hair. He places two strands next to the picture of her father with great care.

"Better late than never," he whispers.

42

Belonging

Simon gets a letter asking him to attend the final Rings & Things. Some kids burned down the Wembley portacabin and thus the session delay. The replacement venue is the crèche at the back of the church at the end of Simon's street.

Wednesday arrives and Simon opens the flaking green door at the side of the church car park and lets himself in. Inside the airy room painted thick with too many coats of magnolia, Tony and Robert are holding hands, sitting side by side in child-sized wooden seats. Simon raises his eyebrows, smiles and they smile back in a warm relaxed way, giving each other's hands a squeeze. Rupert has brought a girlfriend along, which isn't allowed, but it's the last day and nobody seems to mind. Andy is absent — probably spending time with his children over Wembley way. Wilf is slumped over napping. It's so lovely to see some of the gang again.

Simon's hypnotherapist Allyssa is here. He tries to catch her attention by giving her a wave as he takes an empty seat, but she's directing someone behind a red velvet curtain. Simon has given up worrying about everyone being connected. Sonia was right. Losing your livelihood is enough to make anyone paranoid. It's how you respond that counts. Everyone gets a chance to bounce back, to start afresh again. Simon's mother used to call it stickability.

A small black speaker at the front of the stage plays familiar drums: two bars of the intro of "Intruder" are stuck jumping on a record player at the base of some wooden stairs.

The green version of Peter Gabriel's Melt album is leaning against the front left leg of Allyssa's chair. She lifts the tone arm of the record player, the music stops, and she smiles at Liz.

"Gentlemen... and ladies. We've all come a long way." Liz sweeps the room with her eyes and an outstretched arm. "Today's session is one of review but it's also about finding new horizons. Please allow me to introduce Allyssa. Allyssa is a specialist in Family Constellations Therapy, a kind of roleplay in which you'll imagine a member of the group is an ancestor you wish to speak with. Let's all welcome her to the group, and she'll take it away."

Allyssa picks up the chalk and writes BELONGING in big capitals on the blackboard.

"Simon, I want you to initiate todays first constellation session. You will be what's called the seeker. This means you can ask anybody in the room to represent members of your family. Is there anybody you would like to connect with?"

"Yes, my mother and my grandfather."

"Anybody else?"

"No, just them."

"Can I ask you to close your eyes? When you open them, I want you to pick two people from the group, to be your mother and grandfather."

Simon closes his eyes and the broken looping drums stop.

"OK, Simon," says Alyssa. "We must now enter what is called the Knowing Field. You must open your eyes and choose."

Opening his eyes, Simon sees Johan appear from behind the curtain. Simon takes a deep breath as Johan moves to occupy the space between the chairs and the stage. "Yes, Johan," says Simon. "I would like you to be my grandfather and Allyssa you can be my mother."

"Liz, you have to be the facilitator now that I have been chosen," says Allyssa.

"Stay seated, Simon, and close your eyes," says Liz. "Johan and Allyssa will remain standing. We all must focus on the moment for a while."

"I can smell burning, Liz," says Tony.

"Quiet please," says Liz. "Now, Simon, feel free to ask your mother and grandfather any questions."

"What happened in Homberg?" he aims at Johan.

"We used the river to find our way in the moonlight," says Johan.

"I wanted to be a ballet dancer, but I got stuck under the stairs," says Allyssa, guiding a spirit that doesn't belong to Simon's family yet.

A cloud passes over the church and drains the warmth from the magnolia walls of the creche.

Simon's phone pings with a text. It's Sonia. Can you come home? Simon raises his hand.

"Yes," says Liz.

"I'd like to excuse myself, please. My wife is calling. She's not been feeling well."

"We understand. But be aware, you are leaving the Knowing Field," replies Liz before Allyssa can say anything.

"I understand but my real family is waiting for me at the bottom of the street." Simon exits the church creche with a few hurried nods toward his brothers of Rings and Things. With big strides he's back in the flat in two minutes. Inside, Sonia is in the kitchen holding a plastic pen.

"I have news!" Sonia tells him.

"Which way?"

"Simon, we're pregnant!"

43

Two Hombergs

Carrying his laptop to a gig has proved to be far less arduous for Simon. Lugging two boxes of records up three flights of stairs used to set his heart racing. Now all he has to do is arrive early enough to rewire the setup and make sure the bar staff have left enough space for his laptop stand. It's ten minutes to 10 on a Saturday evening and Simon has time to look through the dead man's records while he waits for his DJ shift in the Ilithios Members Club to begin. Through a gap in the shelving Simon spots a homeless man three stories below him on the other side of Portobello Road. It's the same man who stole his vinyl. He's sat on the floor dressed in an expensive camping jacket. In front of him is a bottle of gin; it looks half full. Plenty of fun left in the evening then.

Simon smiles and feels his phone vibrating in his pocket. He leans against the records in the shelving and takes the call.

"Simon? It's Tobias. Don't hang up on me, please."

"I'm about to start work, Tobias," Simon answers after a pause.

"Is everything going to plan?" Tobias sounds concerned.

"I'm not going to die of prostate cancer anytime soon, if that's what you mean."

"The baby, Simon. Is everything on track with the baby?"

"We've had good news, but my wife needs even more injections to keep it that way." Simon's eyes are focused on his laptop screen as he loads up the music file that will start his set. "Serious," start the vocals, and the eighties drum machine kicks in.

"I'm here to make sure this doesn't become a problem," Tobias says as the bassline of Kleeer's "Intimate Connection" weaves between the kicks and snares.

"Wait a second," says Simon. He sets the next track rolling in the software and presses auto synch. He loops the Kleeer track on the vocal, "Spread your wings for the flight," applies the filter, and the track sinks into its lowest frequencies, so he can hear Tobias properly.

"Can you meet me at Biggin Hill Airport at 11 a.m. tomorrow with your passport?" says Tobias. "I would like you to play at a very special event. The fee will be enough to pay for your wife's treatments."

"Why are you all so invested in our baby?" Simon raises his voice over the opening guitar riff of "Stretch Why Did You Do It".

"Be sure to bring your computer and headphones."

"What is this about, Tobias? You're driving me insane."

"Dr Nalbandian is a friend from my college days."

The reception drops out and Simon takes a large gulp from the house wine next to the CDJ.

That night, Simon helps Sonia throw all the unused hormones into the kitchen bin. The little bottles clink as they hit against each other on the way in. He places his hand across her belly and whispers their anxiety away.

At 7 a.m. the following morning they leave the house together. Simon kisses Sonia on the lips and walks with purpose toward the orange sign that marks the Overground station. He climbs down the stairs and paces the concrete platform waiting for his train. He changes for the District line at West Brompton, through to Victoria, then Bromley on a Southeastern train. The 320 bus takes him to the low brick wall entrance of the airport. Its 10:50 a.m. Tobias is waiting for him at the gates in a long black coat and grey Birkenstock sandals.

"Ah, Simon. So good to see you. We need to talk about music, but first to our private plane."

"Private plane? Who's wasting their money on a private plane?"

"Never look a gift horse in the mouth, Simon."

"Where are we going?"

Tobias smiles broadly. "Germany."

A black BMW SUV pulls up next to them and drives them across the concrete airport runway to a King Air B200 turbo prop aircraft. Simon thinks back to the time he could impress Sonia by taking her on trips with him, before the hard times came. But they never travelled in this kind of style.

"Do you think I'm some kind of mega star, Tobias? I come from the underground. I'm only used to free shoes, that's all. Remember?"

"Let us begin the journey with a small glass of Riesling," says Tobias, offering his hand toward the door of the seven-seat prop plane.

The plane is standing resplendent and silver like a cigar tube with square windows cut in. They climb the metal stairs leading to the compact fuselage. The inside is padded with white leather. Three rows of cream-finished seats line the plane. The wine is waiting for them in two shapely Riedell glasses on a polished mahogany table. Simon sits down and Tobias sits alongside him with a long sigh. He takes off his black long coat and the ruby red eyes on his pin badge glint on the lapel of the grey blazer jacket he is wearing underneath.

"I come from a long line of musicians, Simon. My family name is Volkmar but I doubt you have heard of us."

"Volkmar. Sounds a bit familiar, like a dark techno record or something."

Tobias laughs out loud.

"Is that what you are, Tobias? Another one looking for a remix?"

"No, Simon. I'm a gynaecologist."

The gas-driven engines spit into life and the pilot positions for take-off. The revs increase and up they go into the grey cloud carpeted over Kent.

It's a bumpy ride in the small fuselage; the pilot opts to keep the plane low. There's nothing to see. It's cloud from the deck up to twenty thousand feet the whole way through.

"Where exactly are we headed to, Tobias? Somewhere exciting, like Berlin?" Simon tries to hide his nerves by pretending he's on his way to play at a far-flung music festival like the old days. An event he would have been nervous for, but not fearing for his life.

"Allow me to explain." Tobias' voice cuts through the high pitch whirr of the engines. "Mistakes are sometimes hard to rectify, Simon. Do you agree?"

"I suppose it depends on the mistake because a lot of mistakes get made everywhere, all the time, every single day."

"Have you heard of Gee Simon?"

"Can't say I have. Fire away."

"We are travelling to a place where my parents once lived, and their parents before them and so on and so on."

"I'm not sure I've got any Schlager music in my playlist, if that's what you want?" quips Simon.

"I want you to play the music that means the most to you for a few friends and, of course, myself. We are going to Homberg."

"Homberg! Oh shit," the plane hits turbulence and Simon's wine spills over him, Tobias offers him a napkin.

"What the hell happened in Homberg, Tobias?"

"You will see."

The plane banks hard. A break in the cloud reveals a picture-book German town surrounded by lush green fields. The wooden framed buildings cushion a hill ridge that carries a shield wall around the towns round powder tower. They land in a field next to the Friedhof Kapelle, the wheels bouncing on imperfect lumps of soil beneath virgin grass swaying in the wind.

The plane comes to a standstill and the pilot appears from behind the white door separating the cockpit from the cabin. Dr Untermeyer peaks over his sunglasses and takes off his pilot's cap. Simon's throat runs dry. His stomach tingles when Frau Brandt joins him from the co-pilot's seat. Simon grabs his face with his hands and bends over double.

Tobias puts his hand on Simon's back softly. "Come, come," he whispers.

Allyssa is there to greet them, smiling gleefully. The visions unfold like a dream as Simon grips the railing that leads him to the ground.

"Don't worry, Simon," says Tobias.

"We all love to enjoy some good music," Dr Untermeyer interjects, his accent strengthening.

They walk the short distance over to the road that runs by what looks to Simon like a large primary school. A black Mercedes taxi is waiting for them at the side of the road beside the Rathaus. Simon senses the world shrinking, the white painted stucco of the five hundred-year-old wood beamed buildings collapsing in, crushing him.

Allyssa detects his anxiety. "Alles klar, Simon. Alles klar," she tells him with a wink that sends him into a spiral.

The taxi pulls up on Westheimer Strasse and they enter a restaurant with thick, iron-bolted doors. The sign on the door says Philip the Magnanimous. Inside, Simon is introduced to the owner, Heinz Jozt, who greets the party in lederhosen, a white shirt, and a green hat with a pheasant feather poking out. He reaches over the bar and hands Simon a foaming beer.

"Do you seriously want me to DJ here?" Simon's eyes widen.

"Don't worry," says Tobias. "This is not the venue. For that, we go up to the castle. I'm sorry if my friends are giving you bad memories of your operation. Your kind of problem travels unnoticed. Before you know it, it's more than just there."

"You need to tell me what happened here. Why does it seem like everyone is involved in the future of my family? I don't really want to have a party with the man who told me I had cancer." Simon looks over to Dr Untermeyer, who gives him a half smile — a gentle nod as the warm light sparkles on his shaved head.

"Dr Untermeyer removed your cancer as well. But, yes, it must be difficult. I understand the power of memories. Bad ones pass between generations, some say." Tobias places his right hand on the table.

"Bring out the water of the magnanimous, Heinz," Dr Untermeyer shouts across the pristine white tablecloth.

Heinz brings out a large cut glass bowl filled with water. He places it on the table and fetches six shot glasses from an old wooden shelf on the pine-finished wall.

"This bowl is not the original. That was destroyed the night your grandfather came," Tobias says as they lift the mouthful of water to their lips.

"My grandfather?" Simon shakes his head.

"Too many pieces to stick back together again." Allyssa holds her glass up to the light above the varnished pine table.

"He came here?" Simon pokes his finger into the table.

"He never left here, Simon." Dr Untermeyer points toward the castle.

"Not true. I visited Grandfather Jack with my mother in Reichswald cemetery."

"What would you like to eat, Simon?" says Tobias, pointing to the three-foot fish laid out on the serving table. "The pike in jelly I hear is very good, am I right, Heinz?"

"I came here because I need the money for Sonia, for the cytokines in her blood," Simon says to Dr Untermeyer. "Tobias said he's trying to help."

"We know. I sent your wife to Dr Nalbandian," says Dr Untermeyer with a half-smile.

"There are two Hombergs, Simon," interjects Tobias in a firm voice. "This one and the one near Duisburg. Your grandfather bore the letter N on his uniform. He was the navigator and he got it very wrong."

"Got what wrong?" says Simon.

"They bombed the wrong Homberg," says Tobias. "The Fischer-Tropsch oil refinery in Homberg on the Rhine was the target, but instead he bombed our families here."

"What do you want me to say?"

"My grandmother was crushed to death when the wall collapsed onto her under the stairs," Tobias continues, undaunted by Simon's discomfort. "She used to be a ballet dancer you know?"

"I knew he flew — not what, or where," Simon says, feeling exhausted.

"Unter der treppe, Simon," Tobias whispers. "Heinrich, my father's brother, escaped when his mother was crushed under the stairs, and he was found later in the road. The incendiaries lit up Homberg's wooden framed houses and the asphalt melted with the intensity of the flames. Heinrich tried to run, tripped on an upturned curb and got his foot stuck in the bitumen. The road swallowed him up, Simon. My grandfather found a charred figure of his son reaching back to the collapsed stairs where his mother had been. Your grandfather came down in a parachute after his plane was brought down by anti-aircraft fire. It was the second time he had fallen this way."

"Twice, he did this?" Simon steps back with a gasp and his eyes light up in the hearth light flame.

"This pin has your grandfather's name on the back." Tobias unpicks the two-centimetre pin from his lapel and hands it to Simon. "It's a Caterpillar Club pin. Wives used to buy them for their husbands — for those who survived by using their parachute. It was a gift to celebrate life. When Jack floated down to the west of the town, he was captured. The townsfolk marched him through the streets to show him the fires the Lancaster bomber had made. The burned body of Heinrich was still there, unreachable due to the heat. The townsfolk rolled your grandfather up in his parachute, beat him and broke his arm. He was killed with a pistol shot to the head by the father of Hans Jozt. My family tried to stop them, as did Dr Untermeyer's and Frau Brandt's."

"Where did you put his body?" asks Simon, queasy with fear.

"Now we must head to the castle, to hear music," Tobias explains, pointing up in the direction of the hill.

44

Garten Der Schmetterlinge

They walk the stone path on the kerhberg ridge along the shield wall. Homberg's peaked rooves, interrupted by angled beams and white walls, are all pretty below them.

Allyssa walks alongside Simon and takes his hand. "Have you heard of the imaginal discs?"

"The Peter Gabriel album you mean?" says Simon, squeezing her hand. "I'm scared, Alyssa. I tried to trust you, and I nearly let you all the way in."

"Not the vinyl, Simon. The imaginal discs form an amorphous transformation between the caterpillar and the butterfly." Allyssa breaks from Simon, puts her hands together and crosses her thumbs. She shapes her hands into wings.

"I mustn't drop this pin," Simon says, remembering he is still holding the tiny piece of jewellery in the grip of his left hand.

"Let me put it on for you." Allyssa takes the golden badge from Simon and pins it on his lapel. "It won't be hard to imagine, to remember them."

The group stops at the gates of the castle and Tobias pulls a brass key from his blazer pocket. It flashes gold in the moonlight as he slots it into the iron lock and opens the door. He leads them over worn cobbles to an atrium with a glass entrance. The roof struts are black. Inside is gloomy and confused with shapes of vegetation. Tobias opens the door and a rush of warm air greets them. He turns the lights on. The DJ equipment is set up on a table in the middle of the botanic glass house. All around, luscious plants grow in teal, turquoise and Brunswick greens. It was as if a slice of the Amazon basin had been cut out, lifted and flown in.

Dr Untermeyer, Frau Brandt, Allyssa and Tobias take to a table with seats alongside the equipment.

"Are you just going to watch me play?" Simon asks, the fear he felt on the plane digging back in.

Allyssa smiles, almost looking through him. "Play the music that makes the butterflies sing."

Simon starts his set and a blue light brings an ambient glow to the plants that reach up to the beams in the ceiling. The wood is charred and glistens like fresh fish skin. An orange butterfly appears from the high leaves in the oak tree as the music begins.

The Germans sit in the wooden chairs of the butterfly garden, close their eyes and let the music sink in.

Peter Gabriel's "Schnappschus ein Familienfoto" is the first track he plays. A lilac butterfly comes over to Simon's laptop and lands on the edge of his screen. No rhythmic alignment is needed: he's just fading out, fading in. Kate Bush's "Breathing" enchants a thousand butterflies in the room as the garten der schmetterlinge comes to life with the beat of soft wings.

Dr Untermeyer comes over to Simon and gently takes hold of his elbow.

"Come, Simon. Follow me."

The doctor leads Simon through overgrown vegetation,

along a circular stone path to the corner of the garden. An oak tree reaches up to the glass ceiling, the lime green shoots of new growth brush the blackened struts. A small wooden cross is pushed into the ground in the soft tended soil at the base of the tree. Kate Bush's "Breathing" has reached the three-minute mark and is starting to break down. The drums disappear and the fretless bass of John Giblin comes in.

"This is your grandfather, Simon. He was buried here," Dr Untermeyer explains in a low voice, staring into the shadows of the leaves. "Now Jack lives inside the oak tree."

"Was there a fire here?" Simon follows the doctor's gaze up to the charred wooden frame.

"The butterfly garden was built with the wood from the fire damaged buildings next to the road that Heinrich, the uncle of Tobias, was found in."

"Nobody wanted that to happen to him." Simon tears up.

Dr Untermeyer picks an acorn from a low-hanging branch and hands it to Simon. The music comes to a halt and Simon is left alone in silence engulfed by the vegetation. From his pocket, he takes out the paper packet with his mother's hair inside. He ties it to the branch where green-tipped acorns are gathering.

A butterfly lands on Simon's shoulder and spreads its black wings: the centre is patterned with a strip of velvet purple, trimmed in lilac. An orange-patterned butterfly joins the first on Simon's shoulder. Together they beat their wings. One is resting weightless. It opens up for a moment, then takes flight again.

"Simon." Tobias is towering over him. "We want to help you with whatever you need. We seek to replace the spirit of Heinrich. We are committed to solving this spiritual problem. It is for us all to learn — history must not repeat itself again."

45

Speed Bumps, Gas & Air

"We need to go!" Sonia's terse voice pierces the silence, pulling at Simon's film of semi-sleep. "The contractions are getting stronger." Her words are broken by a gasp.

"Oh, God." Simon throws his legs over the side of the bed.

"Don't say anything to the Uber driver — some refuse birth trips," Sonia says, resting her right hand against the bedroom wall, breathing slow and deep.

"When did the contractions start?" Simon exits the bed and heads for the sink to wash his face with cold water.

"I've been up since one o'clock. We have to go now. It's speeding up."

Waiting outside, Sonia's gasps fight for air space as a helicopter passes overhead.

A black Prius pulls up in front of the flat. The driver looks at Simon nervously as he helps Sonia's waddling form into the back seat of the car.

"It's Paddington General Hospital?" Simon says, confirming the digital information passed from his phone to the driver's.

"Yes, sir," the driver replies, his penguin-shaped air freshener swaying on the volume knob on the car stereo.

Simon's eyes meet the driver's in the overhead mirror as the car pulls out. They bounce over the first speed bump and the unborn baby is forced hard onto Sonia's aching cervix. She groans and the driver's flitting eyes look anxious in the mirror.

"Urgh, oh," says Sonia, as another speed bump bangs her body down into the springs of the backseat.

The driver pushes a homemade CD into the dashboard and Fairuz lights up the speakers behind them. Sonia's groans are occasionally landing in time with the fluid sounds of the Lebanon.

"Bil tawfiq, my friends. Good luck!" says the driver as he pulls up outside the Victorian red brick entrance of the hospital.

They exit the cab and enter the lofty halls of St Mary's maternity ward. An elegant powder blue staircase greets them on the entrance to the birthing suites. Simon helps Sonia up the stairs, where they are guided to a cramped assessment room in the reception area.

The nurse welcomes them in her blue uniform. Pushing her black hair behind her ears with a tired sigh she sets about measuring Sonia's vitals.

"You're not ready," says the nurse, gripping her clipboard.

"But she's in agony!" counters Simon.

"The contractions aren't close enough yet." The nurse crouches down and balances on her haunches to tell Sonia the bad news. "You'll have to come back later."

"Please don't send us back. We don't have a car," says Simon, images of bouncing the baby out into a taxi under the west way flashing through his mind.

The nurse calls a doctor. He arrives and takes a blood sample from Sonia's arm. The tests come back twenty minutes later. Sonia is dehydrated. It's enough of a problem for them to stay and wait for the baby to come in the safety of the hospital.

Another nurse arrives to collect them, guiding them through the labyrinth of dark corridors and pine wood doors. "This will be your room," she says.

The nurse holds a door open, revealing the subtle darkness of the birthing suite. A king-sized double with white cotton sheets is flanked by functional pine furniture. A TV rests on a cabinet in front of the bed, twenty-four hour news plays on loop: the Ukrainian army are firing tear gas at protesters in Kiev.

"We're getting the right royal treatment here." Simon lays back on the bed and kicks his shoes off, thinking such relative luxury must come at a price. "How did you pull this off?"

"We get this room because I chose to do it without drugs." Sonia grabs a hold of the TV table, her hair obscuring the battle playing out on the screen.

"Which drugs did you refuse?" Simon rests his hand on her arched back and cups her belly underneath, hanging like an outsized egg.

"The epidural," she says pursing her lips.

"You want to feel pain?" Simon notices the water flowing down the side of the broken guttering in the courtyard. It's starting to rain again.

"Women learn how to adapt to pain before men, and no, I did it so we could get this room," Sonia explains with a quick lift of her supporting hand, turning her palm up then slapping it back down on the table.

"You're an amazing woman," says Simon, chuckling with disbelief.

Sonia's face distorts as another contraction kicks in. Harder, faster, stronger. They get up, leave the low lit room slowly and go for a walk.

Around the hospital corridors they make use of Newton's laws of gravity, shuffling arm in arm. The tall architrave patterned ceilings echo the groans of women walking their babies down from within. Sonia clings to the railings, presses her palms against the eggshell walls and spreads her stance wider as her body begins to take control.

"How are you doing?" the nurse asks as she passes them in the corridor, her footsteps echoing across the shining hand-scrubbed surface of the tiling.

"The gaps are six minutes," Sonia answers without lifting her head; her hair hangs down onto the wooden railing where her white knuckles cling like upended limpets.

"When do we move through to the pool?" Simon wills the final act to begin.

"The pool will be available when the gap is under three minutes," the nurse tells them over her shoulder as she disappears down the corridor.

Sonia and Simon retreat back to the birthing suite. Its dark in their cave, far away from predators and the rattle of the tube trains passing underneath. The hours dissolve, pain the only measure.

Another tall nurse appears silhouetted in the crack of light around the door. She walks over to the bed and sits by Sonia. Together they time the contractions.

"They're close enough," says the nurse. "We can bring you through now."

Simon supports Sonia's arm and they follow the nurse into a bright room full of moulded apparatus-like machines on an assembly line. At the end of the room a light blue, plastic birthing pool sits under dim lighting: a baby jacuzzi. The midwife, a small brunette with her hair tied back, greets them by the sparkling water and welcomes them in.

Sonia walks to the stairs leading to the gently swirling water. She grabs the plastic walls with both hands, legs astride, her body bent forward. Her belly hangs low like a medicine ball was slipped beneath her skin. Light sparkles on the warmed water as the nurse helps her in. Sonia floats like a mermaid bearing gifts, the pain burning at her core.

Five hours disappear. They move out of the pool gingerly and onto the delivery bed. The baby's hair is showing, waters breaking.

"Do you want to touch the baby's head?" the midwife asks in a gentle Yorkshire lilt.

"Just get it OUT OF ME," Sonia screams into the night. Simon can't begin to imagine what it must be like to be split in half by your own kin.

The baby's really coming now, arm bent over his head, skin dark, shiny, and slippery in the half-light of the delivery room.

The nurse wipes the burnt black meconium from the screaming baby's skin. The umbilical cord twists aquamarine, a corkscrew connecting the boy to his mother's life spring. A million yesterdays meet all tomorrow's parties. Now, let them begin: wash away the water, turn everything upside down again.

"The baby has to be taken away for a procedure," the midwife tells them.

"What are you going to do to him?" Simon stands with his hands in an air cradle.

The doctor appears to explain. "We have to make sure he didn't take any of the black tar in."

A second nurse, who arrived in a hurry, looks between Sonia's legs with concern.

"Stitches," is all Simon hears against the aircon and the tinnitus whistling din.

Simon is left in the birthing room. Sonia is wheeled away into theatre. Before they take the baby away he stares at the crumpled face of this thing that just came out fighting to live, and he feels the closest he will ever be to a king. Doused by a shower of chemicals, a newborn sparkle only nature knows lives within. Harmony, sweet harmony, harmony will win.

The nurse leads Simon upstairs to the operating theatre where a freshly cleaned boy named James is waiting wrapped in swaddling. Sonia's legs are spread in stirrups. A doctor has his head down getting stuck in. The nurse hands Simon his son and he cries tears onto him. The baby's hands are foraging, mouth sucking at nothing, trying to find a nipple to latch and some forward milk to bring.

"I know you need your mummy," Simon whispers. He looks up at the partly obscured doctor stitching Sonia back together. "I think the baby wants some milk," he says to the figure behind the white sheets between Sonia's legs.

The doctor lifts his head from the object of his work and Simon sees it is Tobias. Simon grabs hard at the baby and pulls him in.

"I'm sure he does, Simon," says Tobias. "I'm sure he does."

46

Those Were the Times We Had

The winter was dark and warm: too warm by all accounts. Simon has stopped phoning Anne for advice. Listening to her voice on the answerphone made him hurt like he didn't want to hurt anymore.

Sonia went missing for a day after the birth. They found her in a cupboard under the stairs in the operating theatre, still bleeding from the episiotomy and claiming a voice had called for her from the darkness behind the door. Simon had had no choice but to take James home alone the next day and wait for news from the hospital. Offering a broken knuckle to suck instead of a nipple had worked for a little while but he felt useless when his own tears fell on the baby's face again.

Sonia was dropped off at the curb outside the flat the following evening. She had wrapped some ribbons around her ankles like ballet shoes. Simon knew that a different spirit was visiting but he promised himself he would never say another word about those things again.

It's not long before things have settled in. Sonia has taught James to latch when feeding, and the crying has died down.

The bouncer from the Ilithios Members Club got in touch to tell Simon the club had closed, and he had arranged to keep all the vinyl for him. Now it's laid out on the floor of Simon's studio. Around in circles his obsessions with different times spin. Roberta Gilliam's "All I Want Is My Baby" is back in his collection now and Simon can't help but grin.

Sonia hires a car to drive their new family back up north. This time even more of the 50 mph restrictions have been lifted from the motorway. They arrive up the block-paved driveway in silence and wait for Peter to get home. Simon's father is returning from town, after adding two new butterflies to the Hancock museum wall. The names added were Jack and James.

Simon and Sonia climb into the Ford Orion, with the baby in a car seat, and head off on their way to do something for Anne. The sharp sun of an early spring lights the side of the church of St George's, Jesmond, where Jack had helped Anne to walk before his RAF training took him down south and away. They park up in front of the steeple — all around is empty and nature has its way. Peter walks across the church's garden on his own. The droplets of dew catch the dust and the bright green shoots absorb the offering from the urn.

Back in Dillington, the house is exactly the same but gaping empty. Simon is sat next to Anne's wheelchair, which is propped against the vegetable rack in the kitchen. He reaches into the old wooden box of Jack's letters resting on the kitchen table and takes the last one out.

It was written the day before he died.

November 19th
1944

Dear Jean
My last letter rather stressed the physical side of love but,
of course, there is far more to it than that. Apart from the
appreciation of all your qualities, physical, spiritual, it is being
so close to you that by comparison the rest of the people in the
world are as far as the stars.

Simon looks across at Sonia breast-feeding and whispers, "thank you."

Acknowledgements

Edited by Jack Ramm & Elizabeth Allan
Text design by Judith Severne
Thanks to Simon Armstrong @Errant Books
for the guidance
Thanks to Shawn Joseph @Optimum for mastering
the soundtrack and guiding the mixes
Thanks to Michael Skornia @Mocha Produkt
for the design layout
Thanks to Belle Hinchin at Clays
Thanks to Fredrik @Spinroad vinyl
and Cameron @Optimum
Thanks to Emily Robbins @SixtySixProductions
Thanks to Seb Chew for the experience & the advice
Thanks to Tom Rae for the historical research
& proofreading
Thanks to Tobi Kirsch @PassionatePR Germany
Thanks to Lydia Laws & Jenn Nimmo-Smith
Thanks to Jay Cox at On A Plate
Thanks to Simon Sommerville
Thanks to Trevor McNamee for the guidance
Thanks to Ross Clarke for the editorial advice and writing
Thanks to all my artists & friends who took the time
to read & quote

'In a world of Instafame, where only that very moment matters, an era of ephemerality, of the commodification of everything and everyone Simon, and Rae as author work hard to remind us that the past really does exist. And that in the haze of mid-life the future may be harder to find than we think.'
Ross Clarke

'Mark Rae is a true renaissance man – a renowned producer and DJ and now a talented author. This is an accomplished novel; tenderly written, emotional, life affirming and of course – very funny!'
Dave Walker

'A dazzling literary debut from a writer who notwithstanding the subject matter will never be able to resist the inclusion of a 3ft pike.'
Dave Stone

'An honest and insightful odyssey exploring the joy and pain of life and death depicted through the eyes of a self-effacing, insightful and compellingly manic DJ'
Adrian Rebello

'"The soundtrack to our lives" has more meaning for some than others. For some, music is inextricably linked to almost every meaningful moment in our lives and is the lens we present our reality to ourselves. *The Caterpillar Club* illustrates this musical predilection with all of its pitfalls and beauty captured within Simon and Sonia's story.'
Amine Ramer

'One cannot Imagine my joy after reading this book,
to know that Mark has captured and executed his brilliant
gift for delivering the most vivid of narratives just as
masterfully on paper as he does in person.'
Kate Rogers

'A brilliant debut novel that perfectly sums up the
trials of middle-aged DJs and producers while also tackling
grief and loss with a dark vein of humour throughout.
Mark has most definitely added another string to his creative
bow and I really look forward to his future books.'
Stuart Patterson

'I'm so impressed with this book.... although, having
witnessed Mark hold a dance floor in the palm of his hand
it shouldn't be a great surprise that he can do the
same in novel form.
I can also confirm that all references to ageing DJ's
& producers trying to stay relevant in the ever-changing
world of music are 100% accurate.
Great stuff!'
Damian Harris

'In Mark Rae's first novel, he tells of what is clearly,
a very personal and painful journey. He has a great ability
to capture the feeling of personal hardship, that makes
the mundane all around us have meaning, and the intriguing
seem mundane. He also has a strong sense of family and
the value that familial history can have if one is just aware
enough to allow its influence to be felt.'
Chris Stringer

As the first man in history to successfully place a much-needed sense of humour behind dour Mancunian record shop counters, it would only be a matter of time before Mark Rae's wide-eyed wit and arresting story telling skills were forged in print. Extending his own acclaimed autobiography into a wider parallel universe, Mark draws from a vibrant authentic palette which other fantasists would struggle to muster, before flipping the entire canvas to reveal a vista that envelopes all expectations. A book as unlikely as it's frighteningly familiar.
Andy Votel / Finders Keepers Records

'Mark's easy and colourful flow paints scenes which are ultra-vivid, like all great human stories, you are never far away from a laugh or a cry. Wonderful'
Damon Gough / Badly Drawn Boy

Mark Rae was always a great DJ and producer, his relentless energy to find the perfect sample and whip that into a killer beat and rock a crowd as a selector was a given. Mark is obsessed with music and has this amazing knack for associating music with every aspect of his life and everyone else who he's met along the way. For Mark, the narrative of life is defined by music, just like the best music scores work for film. He's now channelled his way of seeing the world into a book that charts the life of a DJ who's had it all but is now coming to terms with age, relevance, mental health, and everything else life can throw at you in such a vivid and honest way.
Colin O'Toole / Film Director / BAFTA Winner

'Mark Rae grapples words as he would a cod.
Firmly, with muscular fingers.'
Andrew Carthy / Mr Scruff

'Mark Rae is pure effervesence, a shining light in our bad
modern world of attention seeking relentless mediocre noise.
A true soul with magic dust.'
Luke Cowdrey / Una Bombers / Elektriks

Wow! I'm not the type to laugh out loud and shed a
tear whilst reading, but this story reaches some of the places
that most others don't.
The Caterpillar Club is a candid insight into the ennui
of the obsessive creative artist who reluctantly has to come
to terms with the final throes of their artistic career
and adjust to a new and uncertain future.
DJ types be warned, this story touches some raw
nerves, Simon articulates much of what you know but
dare not admit to yourself.
Write about what you know – Mark Rae does just this –
the honesty is searing, but as always, very funny.
Justin Only Child / UnaBomber